A Tribute to the Movie,
the Music, and the Man

Ray

Preface by JAMIE FOXX

Foreword by TAYLOR HACKFORD

Screenplay by JAMES L. WHITE

Story by TAYLOR HACKFORD and JAMES L. WHITE

Edited by LINDA SUNSHINE   Designed by TIMOTHY SHANER

Unit photography by NICOLA GOODE

A NEWMARKET PICTORIAL MOVIEBOOK

NEWMARKET PRESS • NEW YORK

10 9 8 7 6 5 4 3 2 1

1-55704-649-2 (Hardcover)

Library of Congress Cataloging-in-Publication Data available upon request.

QUANTITY PURCHASES
Companies, professional groups, clubs, and other organizations may qualify for special terms when ordering quantities of this title. For information, write Special Sales Department, Newmarket Press, 18 East 48th Street, New York, NY 10017; call (212) 832-3575; fax (212) 832-3629; or e-mail mailbox@newmarketpress.com

www.newmarketpress.com

Manufactured in the United States of America.

Acknowledgment of Permissions

We are grateful to the publishers and copyright holders named below for permission to reprint artwork and excerpts from these previously published works. Excerpts and artwork appear on the pages listed.

ARTWORK: **page 6:** © Bettmann/CORBIS; **14:** Photo by Todd Plitt/Getty Images; **39:** Photo courtesy of Showtime Archives, Toronto; **86:** © 1979 William P. Gottlieb, www.jazzphotos.com; **95:** Atlantic Records Archives; **116:** Courtesy of Ahmet Ertegun; **119:** Courtesy of Institute of Jazz Studies, Rutgers University; **133:** Atlantic Records Archives; **159:** Associated Press, AP; **189:** Photo by Frank Driggs Collection/Getty Images; **191:** Photo by Bill Ray/Time Life Pictures/Getty Images; **192:** Photo by Claude Azoulay; **193:** Photo by Hulton Archive/Getty Images; **194:** Photo by Keystone Features/Getty Images; **195:** Photo by Bill Ray/Time Life Pictures/Getty Images; **196:** Photo by Bill Ray/Time Life Pictures/Getty Images; **197** (top): Photo by Bill Ray/Time Life Pictures/Getty Images; **197** (bottom): Photo by Bill Ray/Time Life Pictures/Getty Images; **198:** Photo by Frank Driggs Collection/Getty Images; **199:** AP Photo/Doug Pizac; **200:** AP Photo/Kevork Djansezian; **201:** AP Photo/Greg Gibson; **202** (top): Photo by Tim Mosenfelder/Getty Images; **202** (bottom): Photo by Kevin Winter/Getty Images; **203:** Photo by Todd Plitt/Getty Images; **204:** Robyn Beck/AFP/Getty Images.

EXCERPTS: **"Genius of Brother Ray,"** by Christopher John Farley: © 2004 TIME Inc. Reprinted by permission. *Ray Charles: Man and Music,* by Michael Lydon: Reprinted by permission of Routledge. **"What'd I Say?"** by Ahmet Ertegun: Reprinted by permission of Ahmet Ertegun. **"The Last Words of Brother Ray,"** by David Ritz: Reprinted by permission of David Ritz.

SONGS: **"Anytime,"** by Herbert "Happy" Lawson © 1921 (Renewed) Unichappell Music Inc. All rights reserved. Used by permission. **"Drown in My Own Tears,"** Words and Music by Pat DiNizio © 1958 Screen Gems-EMI Music Inc. and Famous Monsters Music. All rights controlled and administered by Screen Gems-EMI Music Inc. All rights reserved. International copyright secured. Used by permission. **"Hit the Road Jack,"** Courtesy of Ray Charles Enterprises. **"Hallelujah,"** by Ray Charles © 1956 (Renewed) Unichappell Music Inc. All rights reserved. Used by permission. **"I Believe to My Soul,"** by Ray Charles © 1959 (Renewed) Unichappell Music Inc. All rights reserved. Used by permission. **"I Can't Stop Loving You,"** Copyright 1958 Sony/ATV Songs LLC. All rights administered by Sony/ATV Music Publishing, 8 Music Square West, Nashville, TN 37203. All rights reserved. Used by permission. **"I Got a Woman,"** by Ray Charles © 1954 (Renewed) Unichappell Music Inc. and Mijac Music. All rights administered by Unichappell Music Inc. All rights reserved. Used by permission. **"Leave My Woman Alone,"** by Ray Charles ©1956, 1961 (Renewed) Unichappell Music Inc., Trio Music Co., Inc., & Freddy Bienstock Music Co. All rights reserved. Used by permission. **"Mess Around,"** by Ahmet Ertegun © 1954 (Renewed) Unichappell Music Inc. (BMI). All rights reserved. Used by permission. **"The Right Time,"** words and music by Lew Herman © 1965 (Renewed 1993), 1980 Screen Gems-EMI Music Inc. All rights reserved. International copyright secured. Used by permission. **"Route 66,"** by Bobby Troup © 1946, Renewed 1973. Assigned 1974 to Londontown Music. All rights outside the U.S.A. controlled by E.H. Morris & Company. International copyright secured. All rights reserved. **"What Kind of Man Are You,"** by Ray Charles © 1958 (Renewed) Unichappell Music Inc. All rights reserved. Used by permission. **"What'd I Say,"** by Ray Charles © 1959 (Renewed) Unichappell Music Inc. All rights administered by Unichappell Music Inc. All rights reserved. Used by permission. **"You Don't Know Me,"** by Eddy Arnold and Cindy Walker © 1955 (Renewed) Mijac Music. All rights on behalf of Mijac Music administered by Warner-Tamerlane Publishing Corp. All rights reserved. Used by permission.

BRISTOL BAY
PRODUCTIONS

Bristol Bay and the Bristol Bay logo are trademarks of Anschutz Film Group, LLC.

CONTENTS

What set him apart? He was
Ray Charles—*just that!*

—James Brown,
Newsweek, July 21, 2004

WHAT'D I SAY?

by Jamie Foxx

BELOW: Ray Charles in the early 1950s. RIGHT: Jamie Foxx in his amazing transformation as Ray Charles.

I have always wanted to do great things with great people. So when I was offered the role of Ray Charles, I jumped at the chance. It was a dream to play this legendary musical genius who obviously overcame many obstacles as a blind African-American man of his era.

I embraced the huge responsibility of portraying Ray Charles, an icon who has been a force in music for more years than I've been alive. Just meeting the man was life-changing. I was immediately aware of his commanding presence. Ray Charles was a man of great dignity, full of charm, humor, and wisdom. After I played the piano for him, he gave me his blessing. I felt that I was "the chosen one" to help tell his story.

Ray is truly inspirational. He allowed us to tell the story of his struggles to overcome his personal demons. It is extraordinary for a person to be that honest. He was not a perfect man and telling the truth was a mark of his greatness.

I marvel at Ray Charles' accomplishments. He performed at a level that captivated the world. He changed the face of music as a businessman and as an artist. It was pure genius to have this African-American man break color barriers with his music.

Playing Ray Charles is one of the most gratifying and rewarding experiences of my life. I had to wear prosthetics to keep my eyes shut while filming. Although I had the luxury of removing them, my temporary state of blindness made me realize how much we take for granted. I am amazed by the vision, courage, and perseverance that Ray Charles had without sight.

Ray Charles leaves us with so much. His fingerprints are forever a part of our culture. Like Ray, I grew up in the South, I am a Black man and an artist. Because of Ray, I know that I define myself and there is no limit to what I can do.

I am forever his student.

—JAMIE FOXX

UNCHAIN MY HEART

by Taylor Hackford

I first met Ray Charles in 1988 at his RPM headquarters in Los Angeles. I'd come to convince him to allow me to make a feature film of his life story. He came into the room alone, no cane or seeing-eye dog, nothing to aid him except the voice of his son Ray Charles Jr., who was standing beside me. RC side-stepped a table and two chairs, walked right up to me and put out his hand: "Hey Taylor, put some skin in the pocket." Then, evading several other obstacles he sat down behind his desk and shouted, "Did you *see* that Laker game last night? Could you believe that three-pointer Magic sank at the end of the game?" I was stunned—apparently this man could see, which meant that a hoax of major proportions had been perpetrated on the public. Of course, I was wrong—RC was completely blind and had been since he was seven years old. What I came to realize over the next fifteen years—it didn't take us that long to make the film, only to find the financing—was that despite his affliction, RC possessed "insight" that allowed him to maintain control of nearly any situation. He'd promised his mother, Aretha, "always to stand on his own two feet, and never become a charity case with a tin cup in his hand," and he'd kept that promise with a vengeance in a career that spanned seven decades. Not only did he win thirteen Grammys and countless other awards, he was the only artist to ever have top-ten hits in five different categories: jazz, rock and roll, pop, rhythm and blues, and country and western.

As anyone who worked with Ray will tell you, he was not easy. He was a perfectionist who demanded total commitment. I had selected and placed each song in the script to reflect a specific piece of drama in RC's incredible life. Ray had Jimmy White's script translated into Braille and to my great relief he didn't change one piece of music. He did offer to re-record new versions of his records, but I made the decision that we shouldn't mess with perfection. These were masterpieces, and since Ray had been lucky enough to be recorded in his early Atlantic years by Tom Dowd, the finest engineer of his generation, we were able to produce wonderful tracks from the original masters. Yes, we did a bit of enhancement—embellishing horn tracks in a few close-ups—but RC approved everything that our music supervisor, Curt Sobel, did.

When I told him that I wanted to use his best recorded "live" performances for several scenes in the film, Ray personally went down into his vault and pulled out tapes of a great 1964 concert recorded at the Shrine

LEFT: Taylor Hackford and Jamie Foxx on the set.

Auditorium by Wally Heider. From those live tapes we used "What'd I Say," "Hallelujah I Love Her So," "Let the Good Times Roll," "You Don't Know Me," "I Can't Stop Loving You," and "Georgia" from that concert. These tracks brilliantly capture the great Ray Charles Band at a "live" gig.

Of course, archival recordings could not satisfy all the film's musical requirements so we went into Ray's studio and created original material for several important dramatic sequences. I would describe to RC a particular scene, explaining the emotional context or dramatic conflict between the characters, and he would sing and play music that reflected what I'd described. Invariably, Ray was able to get it right in one or two takes.

Having overcome the monumental obstacles he'd faced in his life, RC exuded a confidence that can only come from a self-made man. He trusted his instincts more than anyone I've ever known, and working with him was a major life experience for me.

Ray Charles was definitely one of a kind. He was the best of what America is, and it was impossible not to be inspired by him.

Casting Jamie Foxx

I'd been impressed with Jamie Foxx's work in both *Any Given Sunday* and *Ali* so I recommended him for the role of Ray Charles.

When we met I told him how hard I thought it would be to capture Ray's unique voice patterns and physical movements, but I was most worried about how I could make it look like Jamie was actually playing Ray's complicated piano style.

Jamie told me, "You don't have to worry. I play piano."

I said, "Yeah, so do I, but not like Ray Charles."

Jamie smiled and replied, "Hey, I started playing piano when I was three. I led the band in my gospel church and went to college on a piano scholarship."

I was stunned. I'd known nothing about Jamie's musical talents, which turned out to be prodigious. I began to discover that this extremely intelligent man from Texas was full of surprises and that our collaboration on this film would become one of the highlights of my career.

When Jamie Foxx tells you he can do something, he is not exaggerating, he can do it.

When I introduced Jamie to RC and told him that Jamie was an accomplished pianist, Ray immediately demanded that they sit down at two pianos and jam. Ray had set up two electric pianos, side by side, in his studio, and Jamie took the bait, sitting down to play a little funk and gospel.

Ray matched him for a while and then started playing Thelonious Monk. Now Monk is brilliant, but he doesn't follow any rules; people used to think he was slightly mad.

Jamie didn't have Ray's jazz background so he was in trouble with Monk's complicated figures, and Ray didn't let up on him. He said, "Come on, man, it's right under your fingers, come on, man." The pressure was almost embarrassing. I started thinking that this situation might just blow up in my face.

Jamie Foxx was tireless. This role is probably as demanding as anything you can possibly imagine. In addition to the dramatic component, there was the musical work. It required an enormous amount of time and energy for Jamie to become Ray Charles. Jamie was on the set earlier than anyone else for hair, makeup, and prosthetics and he was the last one to leave. He went home at night and rehearsed his songs; there was a lot of music for him to learn. He is an incredibly hard-working gentleman.

—Stuart Benjamin, producer

However Jamie didn't wilt. He stayed with it until he'd mastered Monk's intricate phrasing. At that moment, Ray jumped up and hugged himself, saying, "This is it! This kid can do it. He's the one."

Jamie just kind of glowed. It was fantastic. I mean, Jamie had the role as far I was concerned, but right there, at that moment, he won the part from Ray Charles.

As tough as he'd been for those two hours, Ray now personally anointed Jamie in the role and from that moment on had only love and encouragement for him. I believe Jamie repaid Ray's trust with a truly brilliant performance.

Acting Blind

When Ray Charles removed his glasses, there was an amazing vulnerability in his face. He allowed me to photograph his eyes, which were always closed, and we used those photographs to make prosthetics for Jamie Foxx to wear in the film. The prosthetics completely covered Jamie's eyes, to the point that he was blind when he wore them.

Jamie wanted to discover what it felt like to be constantly in the dark so for the the month of the film, he was totally blind. Later, we made little slits in the prosthetics so he could look down and see his feet when he walked. Jamie became very proficient in using his hands to guide himself around the room but it was his sense of hearing that truly developed.

Early in the process, I experienced a fascinating example of how Jamie's

ABOVE: The crew and some of the cast members in a group portrait taken in Ray Charles' RPM studio in Los Angeles.

hearing had become enhanced by living in the dark.

We were talking together in a crowded room and suddenly Jamie said, "Quit tapping that pencil."

I wasn't tapping anything and told him so.

He said, "Yeah, you're tapping a pencil and it's so loud that I can't hear what you're saying."

I looked around and, in the back of the room, maybe twenty feet away, a woman was tapping a pencil on the table. Jamie was hearing something no one else could hear. Normally, we are surrounded by noise, but by looking at the person who is talking, we filter out everything except that voice.

Obviously, Jamie was discovering the unique world of Ray Charles and he incorporated those experiences into his work. His interpretation of Ray was uncanny. He didn't "impersonate," he seemed to channel the entire ethos of Ray Charles. It was amazing to watch. Everyone who worked on the film, both actors and crew, came to realize they were witnessing an extraordinary performance. Jamie *was* Ray Charles.

After I'd finished cutting the film together, we went into the studio to do some looping. This is when you replace dialogue that got ruined when, for instance, an airplane passed overhead during filming. The actor comes into the studio, looks at the screen, and re-records the dialogue.

Jamie came into the studio and immediately got very excited when he

ABOVE: Taylor Hackford on the set for the shooting of the scene where RC decides never to play to a Jim Crow audience again and bolsters the civil rights movement.

looked at the image in the screen. "Wow," he said, "look at that, she's wearing a green dress."

It occurred to me that, even though Jamie was on the set for all these scenes, he was only now seeing the actors, the costumes, and the sets for the first time. He had experienced the movie with all his senses, except sight.

ACCURACY

When we finished the script, we gave a copy to Ray Charles and he had it translated into Braille. He had the right to approve the script and I don't mind saying that we were a bit nervous about what he was going to say because his portrayal in the script is not always flattering.

Ray was not an easy human being. How could he be after going through all he experienced? In the script, we made a decision to show many of his darkest moments and portray the pain he experienced as a child. He could easily have rejected our approach and demanded that we change everything.

Amazingly, RC came back with only two minor changes and both of them were inaccuracies. He complimented us on our research (we had gone back to many primary sources) and told us not to change the tone of the script.

Ray was fantastic to work with. Yes, he was tough and demanding but no less than what he demanded of himself: a total sense of excellence and commitment. He gave us an incredible gift. Ray Charles was a great artist, and he allowed other people to be artists also.

INTRODUCTION

MESS AROUND
The Genius of Brother Ray
by Christopher John Farley

When Ray Charles could see, he saw nothing but trouble. As an infant, he could see, if not understand, his father walking out on him and his teenage mother Aretha. At six months, he and his mother moved from his birthplace, Albany, Georgia, to Greenville, Florida, where all he saw was poverty, with his family being even poorer than most, "nothing below us 'cept the ground," as he put it. At age five, he saw his younger brother George drown in a washtub. At about that time Ray developed what may have been glaucoma. He soon found he could stare straight at the sun. By the time he was seven, the sun stopped coming out.

Ray Charles was born with the last name Robinson but dropped it to avoid being confused with the boxer Sugar Ray Robinson. The two had a lot in common—Charles had taken as many hits in life as any pugilist. According to *Jet* magazine, Ray's mother told him, before she died when he was fifteen, "You might not be able to do things like a person who can see. But there are always two ways to do everything. You've just got to find the other way."

From an early age, he was searching. Wylie Pitman, a shopkeeper from round the way in Greenville, had a piano and a jukebox, and he used to invite young Ray to play them both. On the jukebox, Ray would hear blues from Tampa Red, jazz from Count Basie, and pop from Nat King Cole; other times he listened to the box's country or classical selections. On some days, Pitman let Ray bang the keys of his piano. "That's it, sonny, that's it!" Pitman would cry, when Ray was on to something good. At seven, Charles enrolled in the Florida School for the Deaf and Blind in St. Augustine as a charity student and learned to read music in Braille. "In Braille music, you can only read so many bars at a time," he once told *People*. "You can't play it and see it at the same time, so your memory and understanding expand." By the time he was

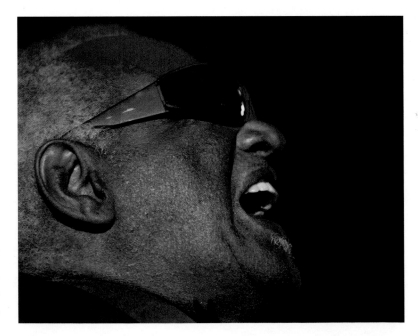

twelve, his fingers were elastic enough that he could arrange big band and orchestral music. Three years later he hit the road as a singer and pianist.

Ray found his sound along the way. Back in Greenville, his mother had taken him to New Shiloh Baptist Church every Sunday. By the time he was signed by Atlantic Records in 1952, Charles was ready to preach. On "I Got a Woman" (1955), he used gospel yelps and yowls for a secular purpose. On "What'd I Say" (1959), he employed the call-and-response of church choirs to generate musical momentum and sexual tension: "Uhhhh!" "Ohhhh!" He didn't need words to get across what he meant, but music writers had a word for his music: soul. "I got criticism from the churches, and from musicians too," he once said. "But I kept doing it, and eventually, instead of criticizing me for it, the people started saying I was an innovator."

Charles has been called the father of soul, but that title is at once too broad and too limiting. He wasn't the first to combine gospel and the blues—but he did it so winningly, you could be sure he wouldn't be the last. He didn't add sex to church music—he just stopped denying it was there. But he was more than a soul provider. Throughout his career, he explored a variety of genres, including jazz and country, imbuing each with his singular grit and charm. His 1962 album *Modern Sounds in Country and Western Music* topped the charts for 14 weeks. Whatever the style, in his greatest performances Charles explored melancholy and then beat it back with pounding piano playing and his broad-shouldered baritone. His rendition of "Georgia on My Mind" (1960) is about more than a state of the union; it turns longing into a state of grace. Many of his other hits, including "Drown in My Own Tears" (1955) and "Busted" (1963), were suffused with despair, but he performed them with such fortitude, they came across as revivifying. Indomitable in life (he overcame a twenty-year heroin habit and fathered [probably] eleven children) and in song (he won twelve Grammys and legions of other honors), he showed that soul was good for the spirit.

In later years he gained mainstream celebrity in the movie *The Blues Brothers* and in Diet Pepsi commercials, but it was always the music that defined his life. Charles raised money for the hearing impaired because, he said, "I can't imagine being deaf. . . To me, it's the worst thing in the world. Imagine never being able to hear music. Most people expect me to help the blind, but I don't think they need help. After all, I'm blind and I'm doing all right." He was doing all right all the way to the end. . . . Charles' legacy should last as long as soul itself. He did his mother proud. He found that other way.

—*Time*, June 21, 2004

Grammy Awards for Ray Charles

1960
Vocal performance, single or track: "Georgia on My Mind"
Vocal performance, album: "The Genius of Ray Charles"
Performance by a pop artist singer: "Georgia on My Mind"
Rhythm-and-blues performance: "Let the Good Times Roll"

1961
Rhythm-and-blues recording: "Hit the Road Jack"

1962
Rhythm-and-blues recording: "I Can't Stop Loving You"

1963
Rhythm-and-blues recording: "Busted"

1966
Rhythm-and-blues recording: "Crying Time"
Rhythm-and-blues solo vocal performance: "Crying Time"

1975
Rhythm-and-blues vocal performance: "Living for the City"

1987
Lifetime Achievement Award

1990
Rhythm-and-blues performance by
a duo or group: "I'll Be Good To You"

1993
Rhythm-and-blues performance: "A Song for You"

LEFT: Ray Charles performing at the Mohegan Sun Hotel Grand Opening celebration, June 21, 2002.

THE MUSIC

HIT THE ROAD JACK
Getting Down the Tracks

Music supervisor, Curt Sobel, has worked on most of Taylor Hackford's films including *Dolores Claiborne, Everybody's All American* and *An Officer and a Gentlemen*, but *Ray* presented many unique challenges.

Every movie has a sound track, of course, but in *Ray*, music is much more than background. Here, music is a major feature; songs are used to move the plot and bring understanding to the story. "The brilliant thing about the script," explains Sobel, "is that you are able to understand why and how the songs were written. When Ray sings 'Hit the Road Jack,' for example, he is telling Margie Hendricks to get out of his life. He'd had enough of her. Taylor Hackford strategically placed this and other songs into Jimmy White's script to help tell Ray's story."

Almost all of the music in the movie is by Ray Charles. "Except for a gospel record Ray listens to in one scene, some incidental source music, and a little bit of noodling on the piano by Jamie Foxx," says Sobel, "most of the music is by Ray Charles. It wasn't always written by Ray, but definitely songs he made famous, and made his own, in his own special stylized way."

Early on the filmmakers decided that Jamie Foxx would lip-synch to the lyrics sung by Charles. Foxx is a brilliant impersonator and might have pulled off imitating Ray's voice, but the opportunity to use the original voice was too enticing. "In the end, we decided that Ray's voice was just too great not to use," says Sobel, "there just isn't anybody who could sing like him."

One problem for Sobel was that Ray Charles' music from the early years did not exist on multi-tracks. Several searches were made through the ABC archives, Atlantic Records archives, and through Ray Charles' own library to no avail. Then, at the eleventh hour, someone discovered a two-track mono version of "I Believe to My Soul" and the ability to tell how this song was recorded became a real possibility.

"'I Believe to My Soul' was recorded in the early 1950s, during a time when Ray's engineer, Tom Dowd, was first experimenting with multi-track tape machines," explains Sobel. "During this particular

BELOW: Curt Sobel and Jamie Foxx recording a big band number. RIGHT: Renee Wilson, Regina King, and Kimberly Ardison perform as the Raelettes. OVERLEAF: The movie spans more than four decades and required many different sets of period instruments as well as a constant shift of musicians and period instruments, amps, and microphones.

I try to put all of me into what
I am singing or playing. If I don't feel
it, I'd rather just forget the whole
business. If I don't believe it myself,
I can't make anyone else believe it.

—Ray Charles, *Downbeat*, July 7, 1960

session, Ray heard playback of the background vocals alone, separate from the music. This was revolutionary for him because, previously, everything would have to be recorded at the same time; band, lead vocal, backgrounds, everything. When Ray heard a playback of the vocal harmonies alone, he decided to lay down the harmonies himself using this multi-track recorder.

"Having separation of these harmonies available to us on the two-track mono version made it possible for Jamie to lip-synch along with the original track of Ray Charles and sing the harmonies himself. Unfortunately, this was the only song where that was possible. In the end, most of the music was record versions of the songs that Jamie had to lip-synch to and synch visually on the piano. Not having separate vocal tracks made the work more strenuous and involved a great deal of practicing so that Jamie could nail both the words and the finger movements. Each take was critiqued in minute detail to determine when the music and the finger playing were in synch or when the film editor would have to cut away to another shot when assembling the footage."

Over a five-day period, Ray Charles was on hand to record some of his

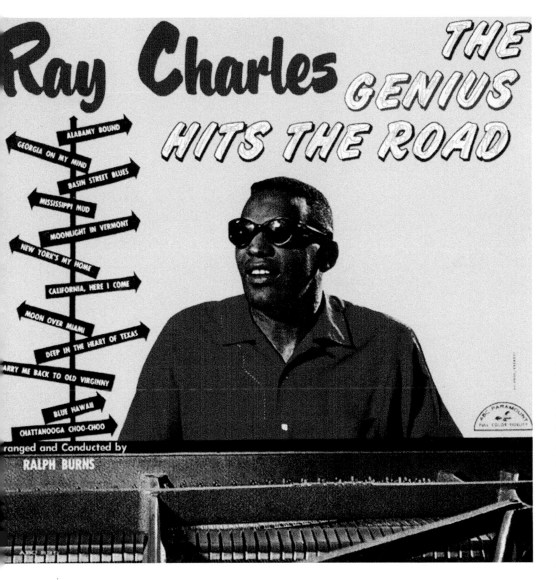

RIGHT: *The original album cover for* Ray Charles: The Genius Hits the Road. *LEFT: A photo of Jamie Foxx is inserted on the album cover. These doctored album covers were used for set decoration.*

In creating the album covers in the movie, we didn't change the style or graphics. We copied them exactly because we knew that people would be familiar with how they looked. We took photos of Jamie in the same poses as Ray appears on the covers. But in a few of them, Jamie and Ray look so much alike what we didn't have to re-shoot them.

—Stephen Altman, production designer

early music, songs like "I Got A Woman," "Drown in My Own Tears," and "You Don't Know Me." He recorded these songs in a way that replicates early piano versions of the music, specifically when he's alone at the piano creating.

There are places in the movie, however, where Jamie Foxx is singing to piano music played by Charles. For Ray's earliest songs, particularly when he was playing in a club or on stage and his style was to imitate Nat King Cole—songs like "Route 66" and "Straighten Up and Fly Right"—Jamie performs a spot-on impersonation of early Ray Charles.

As for the other actors in the movie, some of them were musicians while others required more than a little help from Sobel and his team. "We have some actors who are really playing their instruments," says Sobel. "Bokeem Woodbine, who plays Fathead Newman, is a great example. He played saxophone when he was younger and loved the idea of being able to play it in the film. A coach was retained to show him how to be proficient with his fingering and blowing technique. I made him a CD of the twenty-two songs that he had to perform in the movie, including solos. He was so conscientious, he practically nailed his solos every time."

ABOVE: *Period instruments were used throughout the movie. RIGHT: Ray Charles and Jamie Foxx in the RPM studio in the summer of 2002.*

Regina King, on the other hand, who plays Margie, never claimed to be a singer. "Regina is an incredible actress," explains Sobel, "and in the movie she is belting out songs. I promised her no one would ever hear the production tracks of her. But she is Margie and, when she sings on film, she looks like she is really performing. In her case, that was all that mattered. On the one song, 'Hit the Road Jack,' where she was required to sing live and not lip-synch, I replaced her production vocals in post with a professional singer."

Sobel also worked with the production and prop departments as so much of the movie takes place in a recording studio or on stage. The movie spans more than four decades and required many different sets of period instruments as well as a constant shift of musicians. "We're moving from introducing Wurlitzers to Fender Rhodes to uprights to grands and concert pianos, along with various period horns and guitars. Logistically, it was an enormous job to coordinate everything. Our prop master, Tony Maccario, secured a terrific array of period instruments, amps, and microphones. Hopefully those who know the periods or are familiar with the instruments will recognize that everything is totally authentic."

For Sobel, perhaps the most memorable and magical moment happened during pre-production. On July 12, 2002, an initial meeting occurred between Jamie Foxx, Ray Charles, Taylor Hackford, and Sobel. They got together in Ray Charles' RPM studio in Los Angeles. There, using his digital camera, Sobel recorded Foxx and Charles playing the piano together. "I wanted Jamie to have a visual guide for how Ray moved, how he shifted his body and wore his glasses. The two of them sat at pianos beside one another. Ray would sing and then Jamie would imitate and answer. I swear, we thought we were look-ing at two Ray Charles right there in the room. A few months later, when we met again for our pre-record sessions, using my camera, I stood over Ray's shoulder during the recording of all the takes, this time focusing on his hands. Choosing sections from various master takes, I edited them together and made DVDs for Jamie. This way, he had a visual guide along with the music on CD.

"Jamie is extremely musical and he is a quick learner. He can play jazz, blues, or contemporary music and he picks things up very easily. It is hard for me to imagine anyone else who could've played this role so convincingly."

We had some old songs in the movie that Ray had performed when he was starting out but he had never recorded. We were talking about perhaps bringing in a music arranger and Ray said to us, "Baby, you've got Ray Charles here, why would you bring in some-body else? I'll do the music for you." And he did. . . . I've known Ray for fifteen years and I am still in awe of him. I've been in his office when he said, "I want to sing you something" and he starts singing. It's pretty cool just sitting in a room with Ray Charles and having him sing something for you. Ray was very infec-tious and when you were dealing with him there were certain things that lit up his smile and this movie was one of them.

—Stuart Benjamin, producer

ONE MINT JULEP
My Journey with Ray
by Stuart Benjamin

I met Ray Charles Robinson about sixteen years ago. His son Ray Jr. had contacted Taylor Hackford and me about making a movie about the life of his father. It was a strange dynamic. I don't think that Ray wanted to put a damper on his son's dream of making a movie; however, in 1988, I don't think Ray Charles was really ready to have his life immortalized on film.

Over the years we flirted with several studios that were interested in financing this film. But, for one reason or another, the film never got off the ground.

On one occasion we met in the big conference room at Ray's office. There were four or five studio executives, lawyers, more lawyers, Taylor, Ray Jr., and me. Ray walked into the room without any assistance (he never used a cane), took his seat at the head of the table, was introduced to the others in the room, and proceeded to conduct the meeting as if he was the Chairman of the Board. Actually, he was the Chairman of the Board. He would turn to one participant, address him/her by name, and ask his/her opinion. Turn to another participant, address him/her by name, and make a statement. And so the meeting proceeded until the issue of creative control caused the meeting to adjourn. . . somewhat acrimoniously. However, Ray was in such control of his environment that I guarantee you not a soul in that room left the room believing that Ray was really blind.

Over the years I stayed in touch with Ray. It was our running thing: Someday I was going to get this movie made. Ray would smile, indulge me in my fantasy, and comment that everything happens in its own time and for its own reasons.

Well, about four years ago the forces began to converge. I was an

BELOW: Ray Charles, Taylor Hackford, Jamie Foxx, and producer Stuart Benjamin at the RPM studio in June 2003.

BELOW: Producers Howard Baldwin and Karen Baldwin.

executive at Crusader Entertainment (now Bristol Bay Productions). Phil Anschutz and Howard Baldwin, who were partners in Crusader, believed in my dream of making a movie about the life of Ray Charles. Most importantly, Ray was ready. When you think about it, it cannot be easy to achieve what Ray Charles has achieved and, at seventy years of age, entrust your life story to filmmakers.

We made the deal with Ray. Our relationship had proceeded to the point that "creative control" was not an issue. Trust had superceded creative control. I gave my friend Jimmy White the treatment for the movie that Taylor had written several years earlier, and Jimmy began to do his research and write the script. Taylor, who had been my best friend since college, agreed to direct the film. Ultimately, Jamie Foxx, the only person on the planet who could have played this role, agreed to play Ray Charles.

The best part, however, was Ray's enthusiasm for the process of making this movie. He would read drafts of the script that we had translated into Braille. He would call his old friends to make sure his recollection of events was accurate. Then he would give us notes. But still, I don't think Ray really believed that the movie would get made. At least not until I took Howard and Phil to Ray's office on a Sunday afternoon and Phil said to Ray, "We are going to make this movie."

And we did make this movie. Ray's son Ray Jr., who also hung in with me all those years, was a co-producer. Ray Sr. helped us with the music. He re-recorded songs for us. He found recordings in his archives that had never seen the light of day for us to use in the film. He let us shoot in his studio. He called old friends and told them we would be calling to ask questions about Ray's

life. If something was inaccurate he would tell us and we would make the corrections. However, he never tried to hide from the bad stuff or make us change something that may not have depicted Ray in a favorable light. He wanted the world to get to know him, "warts and all."

At a certain point it became clear that due to his liver disease, Ray would not make it to the release date of the movie. A couple of months earlier, Taylor and I had taken a videotape of the movie to Ray's office and shown it to him. Taylor would describe the setting or the locations and set up the scene and then we would play the tape. Ray loved the film and especially loved the depiction of his mother, Aretha. But seeing the movie on a videotape in his office was not the same as being there for the premiere.

I went by to see Ray a few times those last few months. Although he was visibly frail and weak, he was still mentally sharp and strong. We would talk about the film. I thanked him for having enough faith and trust in me to allow this movie to be made. "Everything in its own time," Ray would say. I guess this was the right time.

Kerry Washington
as Della Charles

Regina King
as Margie Hendricks

Aunjanue Ellis
as Mary Ann Fisher

Sharon Warren
as Aretha Robinson

Curtis Armstrong
as Ahmet Ertegun

Richard Schiff
as Gerald "Jerry" Wexler

Warwick Davis
as Oberon

Denise Y. Dowse
as Marlene Andres

David Krumholtz
as Milt Shaw

Harry Lennix
as Joe Adams

C.J. Sanders
as Young Ray Charles

Larenz Tate
as Quincy Jones

Bokeem Woodbine
as David "Fathead" Newman

Terrence Dashon Howard
as Gossie McKee

Clifton Powell
as Jeff Brown

THE CAST

Wendell Pierce
as Wilbur Brassfield

Chris Thomas King
as Lowell Fulson

Robert Wisdom
as Jack Lauderdale

Thomas Jefferson Byrd
as Jimmy

Kurt Fuller
as Sam Clarke

Terrone Bell
as George

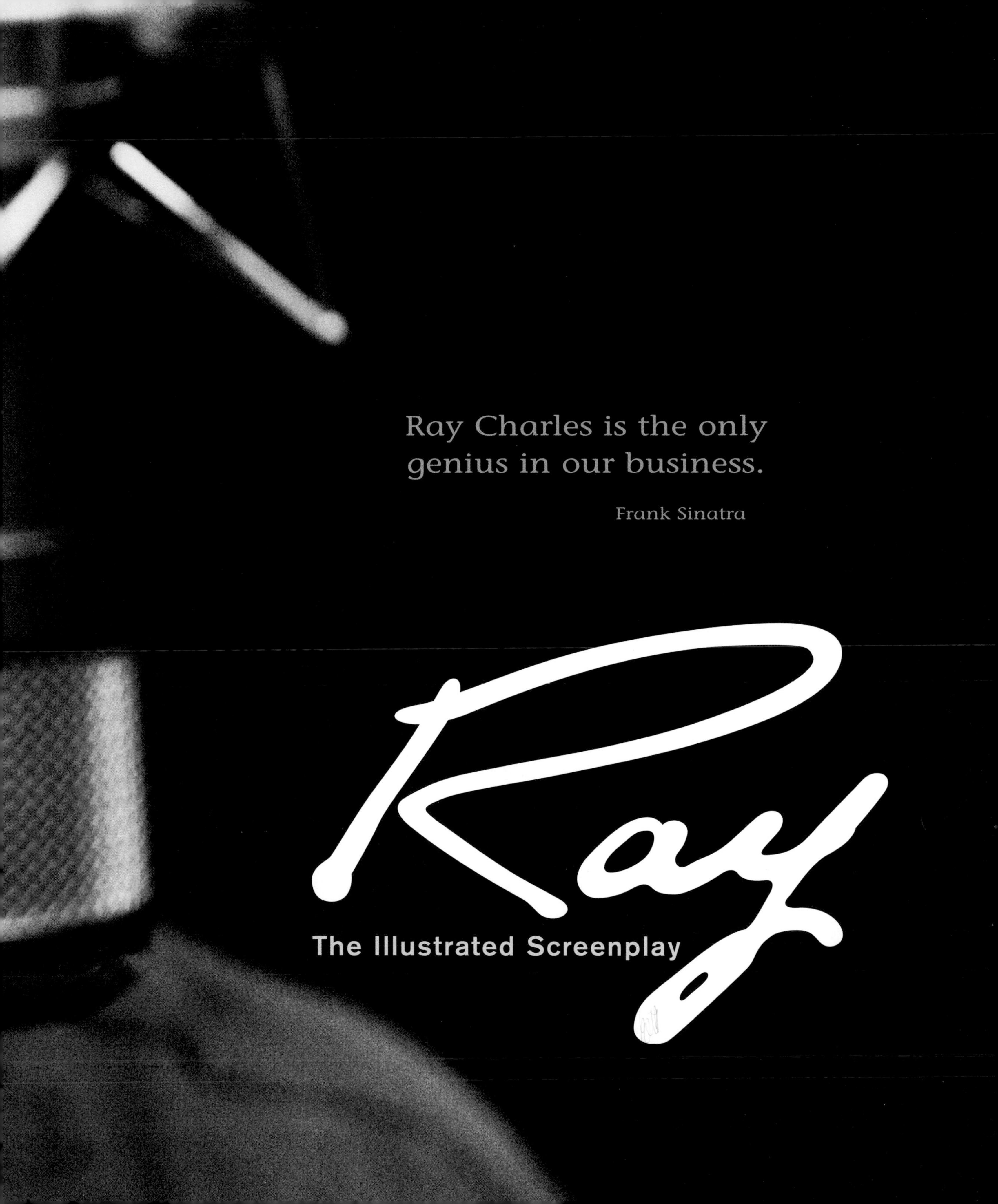

Ray Charles is the only
genius in our business.

Frank Sinatra

Ray

The Illustrated Screenplay

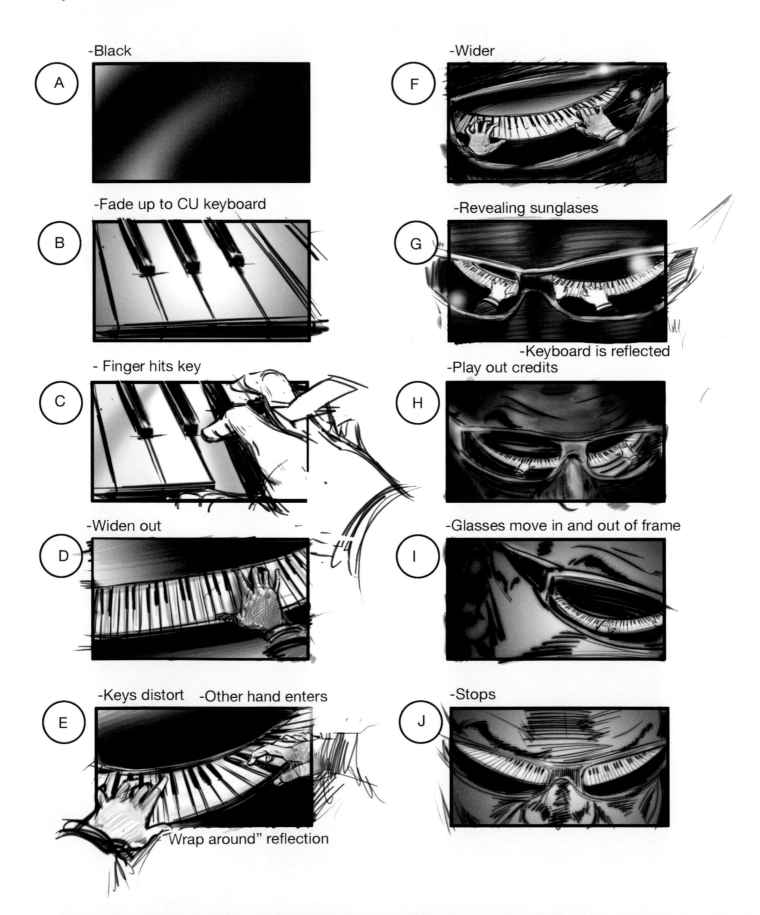

A -Black

B -Fade up to CU keyboard

C - Finger hits key

D -Widen out

E -Keys distort   -Other hand enters

"Wrap around" reflection

F -Wider

G -Revealing sunglases

-Keyboard is reflected

H -Play out credits

I -Glasses move in and out of frame

J -Stops

Black screen.

FADE IN:

BLACK AND WHITE KEYS appear. . . and a pair of dark hands playing the brilliant electric piano intro to "WHAT'D I SAY." Slowly PULL BACK TO REVEAL. . . this is a reflection in a pair of dark glasses. As we savor one of the world's most infectious riffs, SUPERIMPOSE PRESENTATION CREDITS. . . finally giving way to the main title:

"RAY"

CROSS-FADE TO BLACK, THEN CUT TO:

EXT. JELLYROLL, FLORIDA–ROBINSON HOME–DAY–1935–FIRST ARETHA DREAM
A SEA OF WHITE LINEN undulates in a breeze, backlit by the sun. Dark, slender hands sail another sheet over the line,

Storyboard artist Raymond Prado has worked on many of Taylor Hackford's films. The first scene they visualized for *Ray* was the incredible opening sequence where the camera pulls back from a pair of hands on a keyboard to reveal a reflection in a pair of dark sunglasses. This sequence was shot almost verbatim for the opening credits of the movie.

clipping it with a clothespin. REVEAL. . . ARETHA ROBINSON, late 20s, thin and bone-tired in a simple cotton dress. She stares straight at us, her wide, clear eyes unflinching.

ARETHA
I know you done paid the tax, but always remember your promise to me. . . *(beat)* Never let nobody or nothin' turn you into a cripple.

Suddenly, her IMAGE evanesces into BLACKNESS. In a moment, sunlight pierces through, revealing. . .

EXT. ISOLATED COUNTRY ROAD/CAFÉ-BUS STOP–DAY–1948
A blind Negro youth, RAY ROBINSON, 17, stands near a '48 Greyhound in a rumpled suit, a cardboard suitcase in his hands. He waits there patiently, lost in himself as. . .

BUS DRIVER (O.S.)
Rest stop. . . you got 45 minutes! C'mon everybody, you gotta move.

A redneck BUS DRIVER jumps down from the bus. White passengers filing past him. . . heading toward a rural café.

BUS DRIVER *(cont'd)*
There's hot meals an' bathrooms inside. . . Remember, folks. . . we're leavin' at 2:45 on the dot.

A few cars pass by on this isolated country road.

SUPER: NORTHERN FLORIDA–1948

As the whites enter the cafe, five weary Negroes disembark.

BUS DRIVER (cont'd)
There's a window out back for y'all to buy sandwiches, an' I suggest you make good use of them outhouses. . . Ain't nothin' but bushes for ya in the Carolinas.

As the "coloreds" head out back, the driver notices Ray.

BUS DRIVER (cont'd)
Can I help ya, son?

Ray's eyes, covered by sunglasses, may be sightless, but he focuses intensely on the driver, handing him his ticket.

RAY (holding out a ticket)
Yes, sir.

BUS DRIVER (glancing at the ticket)
Seattle. . .? Who you ridin' with?

RAY
Nobody. . . just me.

BUS DRIVER
Boy. . . I can't be takin' responsibility for a blind nigra travelin' 3,500 miles alone.

RAY
I paid for this here ticket and it says you gotta take me to Seattle.

BUS DRIVER
Don't you be smartin' off to me, boy.

The young man lifts his sunglasses, revealing scarred eyes.

RAY
With all due respect, sir, I got a right. . . I may've left my eyes on Omaha Beach, but I ain't askin' Uncle Sam for no charity. I got a job waitin' for me in Seattle.

BUS DRIVER (immediately softens)
You were at Normandy. . .?

RAY
A coxswain shuttlin' troopers to the beach. . . we took a direct hit.

BUS DRIVER
Sorry, son. . . I'll keep an eye on ya myself. Take a seat in back.. . .

As Ray moves forward past the driver, we see a slight smile.

EXT. GREYHOUND BUS–DAY–STOCK–1948–SUPER CREDITS
A SERIES OF SHOTS as the bus rolls through the South.

INT. GREYHOUND BUS–DAY–1948–CREDITS CONTINUE
Dolly down the aisle as the WHITE POP SOUNDS of 1948 America echo from the bus radio. Most of the passengers are paired up: a young soldier with his new bride, mothers with their kids, strangers making friends. But three rows from the back, a chain stretches across the aisle holding a "COLOREDS ONLY" sign. Ray sits with the five other Negro passengers. He's silent, motionless. . . lost inside himself.

EXT. BUSTLING CHICAGO– DAY–1948
The Greyhound Silverside cruises through an intersection.

INT. GREYHOUND BUS–DAY–1948
The bus driver takes down the "Colored Only" sign. He turns to Ray, who is sitting alone.

BUS DRIVER
Son, we got a new bus driver to take you to Seattle. I told him to keep an eye on you.

INT. GREYHOUND BUS–DAY–1948
Four drunk marines stumble down the aisle, passing Ray and flopping onto the back seat.

EXT. BUS ROLLING ACROSS MIDDLE AMERICA–TRANSITION TO NIGHT–1948

INT. GREYHOUND BUS–NIGHT–1948
One of the Marines strums a ukulele and sings, "Mairzy

LANDMARK MOMENTS

After gigging around northern Florida as a teenager, Ray Charles considered himself one of the best musicians in his community. Then he tried to take the next step up the ladder by auditioning for a nationally known band leader named Lucky Milander. However, Milander rejected him saying Ray wasn't good enough to be in his band. Ray told me this story and said that he could still feel the sting of Milander's words: "not good enough." At that moment RC realized that if he was going to grow as an artist, he would have to leave Florida even though he had a comfortable life, especially for a blind man. He had a girlfriend, a roof over this head, and a good steady job, but that wasn't good enough for Ray Charles.

He didn't want to go to New York or Los Angeles because he felt those cities would be too big and too tough at the beginning. So he asked a friend to stretch a string out on a map and find the furthest place from Tampa, Florida, which turned out to be Seattle, Washington. It was the late 1940s when Ray got on a Greyhound bus, alone, and traveled across the country.

When he arrived in Seattle, he got off the bus, found a hotel, went to a club, and won a talent contest that very night. He was only seventeen years old and, oh yes, he was blind. The movie opens with these scenes because it is certainly a landmark moment in Ray's life.

—Taylor Hackford

That Ray Charles chose to rely on himself at 17 is noteworthy in itself: few reach this turning point so young, fewer still who are blind. It also stands as a first clear example of many such choices to come. . . . . [W]hen faced with dependence one way, independence another, Ray Charles will, with rare consistency, choose independence. Again and again he would move away from people and places previously known, cut himself out of webs of the past when they threaten his freedom in the future. Independence became in time an ingrained habit of the man, an element of his makeup that some found grouchy; others cold-blooded. The darkness he lived in revealed one plain fact: humans live and die one by one, all ultimately alone. With the passing years he became more and more determined to reap what advantage he could from facing that truth without flinching.

—Michael Lydon, *Ray Charles*, 1998

Doats." He camps it up. . . making the others laugh.

SOUTHERN MARINE
Okay, now do a country song.

NORTHERN MARINE
Country? We're not some hicks. . .

SOUTHERN MARINE
Hick. . . ? Come on, Reggie, let's educate this northern clown. Show 'im what *real* music is. . . What shall we do?

REGGIE
Let's do "Anytime."

SOUTHERN MARINE (*attempting to sing*)
Anytime, you're feeling lonely. . .
anytime you're feeling blue. . .
(*beat*) Damn. I forget the rest. . .

Suddenly, from the seat in front of them, a soft male voice picks up the song.

RAY
Anytime you feel downhearted,
That will prove your love for me is true

The Marines can barely see Ray, sitting in the shadows. . . but they like his sound, and sing along.

RAY & THE MARINES
Anytime you're thinkin' 'bout me,
that's the time I'll think of you.
Anytime you say you want me back again,
that's the time I'll come back home to you.

The Marines end with a flourish, applauding themselves. The southern Marine leans over to congratulate Ray.

SOUTHERN MARINE
That was great. Thanks, fella. Hey, what's with the shades?

RAY
I'm a jazz musician.

> ### I never wanted to be famous, but I always wanted to be great.
>
> —Ray Charles, liner notes,
> *The Genius of Soul Live!*

SOUTHERN MARINE
A jazz musician singin' Eddie Arnold?

RAY
Hey man, music's music.

Ray turns away as if he's looking out the window. Ad libs from Marines.

CUT TO FLASHBACK:

INT. EMPTY COUNTRY & WESTERN BAR–DAY–1947
BILLY RAY—big, white, and country—rehearses his band, the FLORIDA PLAYBOYS. One girlfriend sits idly by, smoking.

BILLY RAY
Alright boys, settle down. I'm sick and tired of Til's dead ass being late. We're gonna work on "Sun Gonna Shine" without him.

Suddenly, their guitarist, TIL, 30s, leads Ray through the front door. Billy Ray is not happy.

BILLY RAY (*cont'd*)
Til, what in the hell do you think you're doin'?

TIL
Don't get your feathers ruffled now. I met this ol' boy over at the OC at Clark Field. He plays a helluva mean jazz piano. . .

RIGHT: One of the first known photographs of Ray Charles, before he began wearing his trademark sunglasses, circa late 1940s.

BILLY RAY
I don't care if he whistles Dixie out his ass, he ain't doin' it here.

TIL
Come on, Billy, ain't no skin off your nose to let him show you what he can do. We've been looking for a piano player for over a month now.

BILLY RAY
Not interested.

He turns away. Ray just stands there, intimidated yet standing his ground.

RAY
Sir. . . ?

BILLY RAY
Boy. . . are you blind?

RAY
Yes, sir, since I was seven.

A few laughs.

BILLY RAY
Let me help you out then. This is a country band. . . we don't play no boogie-woogie.

RAY
I know. . . I love country music.

Billy Ray just stares at Ray.

BILLY RAY
You ain't gonna quit, are you? *(off Ray's silence)* Awright. What do *you* like about country music? Go on. . . tell me.

As he sits he hits some keys. Ray's head jerks around at the ECHO of the hollow wood, the slight HUMMING of the strings — MAGNIFIED, in his ears, far above the laughter.

RAY *(steeling himself)*
Well. . . I like the stories.

BILLY RAY
The stories.

RAY
Yeah. 'Bout the way people love. . . the way love kicks 'em around. Or how the world weighs on you sometimes. . . makes you feel small. Like you might as well give your soul to God, 'cause your ass sure belong to Him.

Ray heads toward the piano. He reaches out, touches the wood. Billy Ray and his boys watch him closely now. Ray caresses the bench, sits down.

BILLY RAY
You sure you're blind. . .?

Without a word, Ray begins to play, and he's exquisite from the opening bars of "Anytime," the same mournful country ballad. One by one, the rest of the Playboys join in.

TIL
Billy, I think you're outvoted.

BILLY RAY
I'm warnin' ya, Til, one hint of trouble and your blind nigra's outta here. An' I'm gonna put some goddamn sun glasses over 'em eyes before he scares people to death.

Till reaches over and snatches a pair of cat's eye sunglasses off the girlfriend's face. He puts them on Ray—a kind of coronation—as he keeps on grooving with the Playboys.

EXT. GREYHOUND BUS–NIGHT–1948
The Silverside glides to a stop. The door opens.

BUS DRIVER (V.O.)
Seattle! Seattle, Washington!

INT. GREYHOUND BUS–NIGHT–1948
Ray wakes up, rubbing the sleep from his eyes. He listens to the sounds of a new city. . . happy, excited.

EXT. THE ROCKING CHAIR CLUB–NIGHT–WET STREETS–1948
A cab swooshes to a stop on the wet street. . . and Ray gets out. His "sonar" instantly picks up the sounds of laughter drifting from the club. He starts toward it. . . when he hears another sound: A jazz trumpet, blowing an intricate riff. Ray is drawn to a black 15-year-old kid, sitting on the curb.

RAY
That's Diz. . . "Emanon."

KID (a challenge)
What's it mean spelled backward?

RAY
"No Name."

The kid smiles now, approaching him.

KID
What ax you play. . .?

RAY
Piano. I jes' blew in from Tampa, Florida. . . me 'an

my partner Gossie McKee come up here to fatten up our style. Cop some licks from some more experienced cats, you dig?

KID (laughs)
Yeah, I dig, but tonight is "no talent" night here at the Rocking Chair. Now, Chew Berry's over at The Black an' Tan. Wanna check him out?

RAY
Another time, brother. I gotta meet my man Gossie inside.

KID
You know what, why don't I take you inside, show you around. . . just like my place. . . (leading Ray off) So what's your name?

RAY
Ray Robinson.

KID
I'm Quincy. Quincy Jones.

They reach the door to the club, covered by a BOUNCER.

> I couldn't figure out how eight horns—four trumpets and four trombones—could play together at the same time and not play the same note. [Then Ray Charles] hit a B-flat-seventh chord in root position and a C-seventh above that, and there it was, the eight-note chord with the Dizzy Gillespie sound. He hit that thing and the whole world opened up. Everything from then on made sense.
>
> —Quincy Jones, *Jackson Street After Hours: The Roots of Jazz in Seattle*, 1993

QUINCY *(cont'd) (to the Bouncer)*
Gerry, I want you to meet my man, Ray. We're meeting his friend, Gossie McKee, inside. I figured I'd show him around.

BOUNCER
Don't start with me, Q. He can come in, but not you. Vice is up my ass for lettin' you underage kids in. Get outta here, Q.

QUINCY
He's blind. . . I gotta show him in.

The bouncer won't let Quincy in. Ray turns to go in, but Quincy shouts after him.

QUINCY *(cont'd)*
Hey, Ray Robinson!

RAY
Man, don't be shoutin' my name like that. . . it ain't cool. *(smiling)* If you want to get my attention, just call me 6-9, from now on.

QUINCY *(charmed)*
Okay, 6-9, when do I get to hear you play?

RAY *(smiling slyly)*
That may cost you. *(to Bouncer)* Gerry, could you show me in?

Ray steps into the club leaving Quincy intrigued.

CUT TO:

INT. THE ROCKING CHAIR CLUB–AFTER MIDNIGHT–1948
CLOSE-UP: OBERON, the dwarf MC of The Rocking Chair, purrs to the audience.

OBERON
Welcome all you cool cats an' fine felines. . . you've come to the place where the SophistiCats an' Hipsters hang their Be-Bop hats. . .

Oberon commands the tiny stage of this SEEDY DUMP. Waitresses flit about, serving the mostly black clientele.

OBERON *(cont'd)*
. . . snuggle up an' come near, for this is Talent Night at

In Seattle, Ray Charles cut his first record, "Confession Blues," and formed what would become a lifelong friendship with Quincy Jones. In the two years he remained in Seattle, Charles performed regularly at the black Elks Club on Jackson Street and at the blues-oriented Rocking Chair Club on 14th off Yesler. Charles recorded "Rockin' Chair Blues," a tribute to Seattle, just before moving to Los Angeles in 1950.

The Rocking Chair. *(tossing sand on stage)* Let's hear it for Dancin' Al!

An old time hoofer jumps on stage and begins a slow shuffle.

INT. THE ROCKING CHAIR CLUB BAR–NIGHT–1948
AT THE BAR, Ray is hungrily eating a bowl of chili. . . MAR-LENE ANDRES, black, 40s, pleasingly plump, sizes him up.

MARLENE
Gossie's been cattin' 'round with one of my waitresses since he got here. *(checking Ray out)* He never told me his partner was a blind 'Bama boy. . .

Ray ignores Marlene as Oberon scurries up, whispers to her:

OBERON
Demurs just called. . . Thurmond's sick.

MARLENE
What 'bout Sassy?

OBERON
Flat tire.

MARLENE *(turning to Ray)*
Okay, 'Bama. . . why don't you get on up there an' show me what you got?

RAY *(a slow burn)*
I ain't no 'Bama. . . an' I'm not no amateur neither.

MARLENE
This is the only audition you're gonna get, puddin', so get up there or you and Gossie can haul your asses back down south!

Ray senses she's not bluffing. He hears the audience laugh derisively as they harass Dancin' Al. . . and he goes cold.

RAY *(nervously)*
Y'know. . . I wasn't really prepared to do my thing, tonight.

OBERON
Here, smoke some of this.

Oberon hands Ray a joint. Ray inhales and coughs.

RAY
This ain't tobacco. . . .

OBERON
Hold it in. It'll calm you down.

Ray takes a long pull on the joint and holds his breath.

MARLENE *(to Oberon)*
Get on up there and introduce him. *(taking Ray's arm)* Let's go, 'Bama.

CUT TO:

INT. THE ROCKING CHAIR CLUB STAGE–NIGHT–1948
A spotlight illuminates Oberon on stage.

OBERON
Now, I got somethin' special for you satin dolls, an' I don't mean Oberon's big thunder—that's for another show. *(hoots from the women)* We got some new blood for ya, straight off the bus from Florida. . . I give you Ray, *"Don't Call Me, Sugar,"* Robinson!

No applause as Marlene helps Ray onto the stage, then abandons him. Disoriented, he reaches out for the piano chair. Ray finds the chair but knocks it over.

RAY *(disoriented)*
Okay, folks. . . how's everybody doing tonight?

MAN IN AUDIENCE
Better than you. . .

RAY
Whatcha wanna hear?

A tough crowd. From the wings, Oberon appears, righting the bench and sitting Ray down on it. It's his first solo gig in a real jazz club, and he's terrified. CLOSER ON Ray. . . as we:

FLASHCUT TO BLACK:

INT. ROBINSON HOME–NIGHT–1935–SECOND ARETHA DREAM.
Aretha sits next to an oil lamp sewing. She looks straight at us. . . a mischievous smile on her face.

    ARETHA
How 'bout a little Charles Brown. . . ?

        FLASH CUT FROM ARETHA'S IMAGE BACK TO:

INT. RAY ON STAGE AT THE ROCKING CHAIR–NIGHT–1948
Ray begins singing Charles Brown's "Driftin' Blues." Ray's fingers heat up the keyboard. He continues singing for another moment.

    RAY
So if you like Charles Brown. . . is Nat King Cole in the house?! *(singing and playing)*
Well if you ever chance to motor West, just go my way, the highway that's the best. . . Get your kicks on Route 66. . . .

Ray's version of Nat Cole's "Route 66" is a perfect imitation. The delighted audience actually applauds.

AT THE BAR, Marlene is impressed. She looks down at Oberon.

    MARLENE
The 'Bama ain't bad. . . .

    OBERON
I'd say he saved our asses.

GOSSIE McKEE and a DISHWATER BLONDE enter.

I never considered myself part of rock and roll. My stuff was more adult. It was more difficult for teenagers to relate to; my stuff was filled with more despair than anything you'd associate with rock and roll. Since I couldn't see people dancing, I didn't write jitterbugs or twists. I wrote rhythms that moved me. My style requires pure heart singing.

—Ray Charles, *The Los Angeles Times*, June 11, 2004

MARLENE
Millie, quickie's over, back to work.

Gossie ambles up to her.

GOSSIE
What the hell's Ray doin' up there?

MARLENE
Auditioning for you, Gossie.

GOSSIE
He ain't no good without me.

MARLENE
How would you an' the 'Bama like to do a week here?

GOSSIE
I'm all ears.

MARLENE
I know a bass player. Jazz trio could score big. . . with the right manager.

GOSSIE
Manager?!

MARLENE
Don't be small-minded, now. Sometimes you gotta give to get.

GOSSIE *(sighs, nods)*
So how much I gotta give?

MARLENE
Say 25 percent. . . *but* I'll be gettin' you other gigs.

GOSSIE
An' what do I get?

MARLENE
What do ya need?

GOSSIE
Double scale as leader, plus 10 percent.

MARLENE
What about the 'Bama?

GOSSIE
He's green as a blade of grass. I'll handle him.

MARLENE *(watching Ray)*
Yeah, he's green. . . you right 'bout that. *(beat)* Listen, Goss. . . don't worry 'bout a hotel for the 'Bama. He can flop at my place.

Gossie laughs knowingly. Oberon, troubled by their conversation, slides off his stool and waddles back to the stage. . . where Ray is knocking 'em dead.

GOSSIE
You don't ever change.

MARLENE
I'd disappoint you if I did.

Back to stage.

RAY
Louis Jordan? I know you're 'round here someplace. . .

47

There's a story that when Mozart was invited to hear a choir rehearsal, he asked to see the score. The choir director said no, but at the next rehearsal Mozart gave the choir director a copy of the score he had written out from memory. I'm not exaggerating: Ray Charles has that kind of mind. If he hears something once, he can dictate every note you played.

—Renald Richard, bandleader, Michael Lydon, *Ray Charles*, 1998

Ray starts singing "Caldonia." The crowd joins in, with people answering him.

EXT. SERIES OF STOCK SHOTS OF SEATTLE–DAY–1948

INT. MARLENE'S HOUSE–BATHROOM–DAY–1948
CLOSE UP: WATER gushes into a glass TILT UP TO Ray, body glistening with perspiration as he gulps the water down.

> **MARLENE** (V.O.)
> Ray. . . you comin' back to bed?

DROP FOCUS to Marlene in the background, lounging in bed.

> **RAY**
> Yeah, I'm gettin' some water.

> **MARLENE**
> Good. . . 'cause Mama ain't finished.

In disbelief, Ray pours the remaining water over his head.

**INT. THE ROCKING CHAIR CLUB–A PACKED
HOUSE–NIGHT–1948**
CLOSE-UP: a black man's graceful fingers caress bass strings.

OBERON (V.O.)
Guys an' dolls. . . what we got for you oughta be against the law!

The SKINNIEST BASS PLAYER in Seattle joins Ray and Gossie on the intro to "Straighten Up And Fly Right."

OBERON (cont'd)
For the first time—anywhere—hit it. . . Let's hear it for the McSon Trio!

Ray breaks into a dead-on imitation of Nat Cole's "Straighten Up and Fly Right."

INT. MARLENE'S HOUSE–BATHROOM–DAY–1948
DRIVING RAIN beats against the bathroom window. Camera pans down to Ray, fully clothed, sitting on a closed toilet.

MARLENE (V.O.)
Ray, when you comin' out?

RAY (irritated)
In a minute!

MARLENE (V.O.)
Hurry up, Mama's gonna give you some more blackberry cobbler.

Ray sighs and flushes the toilet. MUSIC CONTINUES as we. . .

CUT TO:

EXT. ROCKING CHAIR CLUB–DAY–1948/1949
A PHOTO OF THE McSON TRIO on the club marquee. VFX: STICKERS WIPE ACROSS FRAME—"Extended Thru Christmas," "Back by Popular Demand. . . ."

INT. MARLENE'S HOUSE–BEDROOM/1949–DAY–MUSIC CONTINUES
CLOSE UP ON RAY, devouring a piece of chicken. Suddenly, Marlene sits up and pulls him down, OUT OF FRAME.

EXT. ROCKING CHAIR CLUB MARQUEE–DAY–1949
A MONTAGE OF STICKERS WIPES ACROSS THE McSON TRIO'S PHOTO on the marquee as the MUSIC CONTINUES: "4th of July Party featuring our Favorite McSons"—"Engagement Sold Out"—"Extended thru Thanksgiving."

INT. MARLENE'S HOUSE–BEDROOM–DAY–1949
Ray packs his suitcase. Marlene is in the bathroom, putting on her eye make-up.

RAY
Marlene, Gossie's car ain't gonna make it. We should take yours.

MARLENE
I ain't lettin' Gossie drive my car. . . he'll wreck it.

Something's on Ray's mind. He packs in silence for a moment.

RAY
Five bucks a day ain't cuttin' it. How come we can't get paid after each gig. . . ?

MARLENE
'Cause you boys'd spend everything you make. The clubs send the checks to me, so's I can bank 'em.

RAY
But. . . I want to see my own checks.

MARLENE *(an edge)*
You don't see, Ray. You're blind. Or did you forget that. . . ? *(putting on her coat)* Why don't you go out on your own. . . see how well you do?

Ray is silent. He'd love to go out on his own. . . but he's afraid. Marlene smiles, gives him a peck and leaves.

Miserable, he stuffs a shirt into his suitcase. . . and WATER BEGINS TO SEEP THROUGH THE MATERIAL. He reaches under the clothes, searching frantically for the source, revealing. . .

THE WET, LIFELESS BODY OF A LITTLE BLACK BOY.

Ray stumbles backward, muffling a cry of terror. His clothes are completely dry. . . . In the distance, a door slams.

QUINCY'S VOICE (O.S.)
Hey 6-9! . . . Anybody home. . . ?!

Quincy bounds into the room, brimming with excitement.

QUINCY
6-9. . . Lionel Hampton just asked me to hit the road with him. Lionel Hampton, man!

RAY *(trying to cover)*
So what you doin' here?

QUINCY
Exactly. Dig this. His wife threw me off the bus. . . told me to come back when I start shavin'. Can you believe it?

Ray gropes around in his suitcase. . . but the boy is gone. His clothes are completely dry.

RAY
Can you close that thing for me. . .

Ray smiles, but his face is haunted, distant.

QUINCY
What's wrong with you? You got two hands..?

RAY
I got two feet, too. . . just close the bag.

QUINCY *(obliging him)*
Sure. . . I think the woman is crazy. She thinks I'm gonna outshine everybody when I play my horn. . .

They exit, ad libbing.

EXT. AERIAL SHOT–CEDAR FORESTS–DAY–1949
The woods fringing the Puget Sound are dark and deep. Evergreens tremble in the wind.

EXT. WASHINGTON STATE HIGHWAY–DAY–1949–MUSIC CONTINUES
Gossie's old clunker has broken down. Ray and the Skinny Bass Player are under the hood while a pristine Gossie watches.

RAY
So, what do you think it is, Milt? The carburetor?

GOSSIE
It just overheats sometimes. Somebody's gonna come along.

A car passes. Gossie tries to hail it, but it passes on.

RAY
I need my own place, Gossie.

GOSSIE *(shrugs)*
Why? Ya got free rent, baby.

RAY
Like hell it's free.

GOSSIE
She doin' it to you? Hey. . . at least we're workin'. That's more than a lot of cats can say.

RAY
Yeah. Doin' the same ol' same old. . . .We gotta be experimentin'.

GOSSIE
Ray, you good, but you ain't no Thelonious Monk. . . *(laughs)* Hey Milt, he thinks he's Thelonious Monk now. . . But I bet you could imitate him!

RAY
Is that all we are, some imitators?

Gossie hesitates. . . sensing how much this bothers Ray.

> The blues and spirituals are all about . . . the ability to look at things as they are and survive your losses, or not even survive them—to know your losses are coming. Charles sings a kind of universal blues. It is not self-pity, however, which you hear in him, but compassion.
>
> —James Baldwin, *London Sunday Times*, May 12, 1963

GOSSIE
Ray. . . we got a sound that's working, man. And Marlene wants us to keep it that way. How do you think she's bookin' us into all these white clubs? 'Cause we got a sound those people can relate to. . .

RAY
But at the Negro clubs, we could play what we relate to.

GOSSIE
What about that knot in your pocket? Can you relate to that? *(letting that sink in)* Look. . . right now, we're ridin' down easy street with the top down an' the wind blowin' in our hair. Why mess with a good thing. . . ?

Ray has no answer to that. . . .

GOSSIE *(cont'd) (winking at the Skinny Bass Player)*
Just keep layin' that pipe, okay? Marlene's gonna make us all rich. . .

Another car passes. Gossie is not successful in flagging it down.

INT. THE ROCKING CHAIR CLUB–NIGHT–MUSIC ENDS–1949
Ray and the McSon Trio are on stage, playing the last bars of "Straighten Up" to a packed house. Oberon jumps on stage.

OBERON
Back from their triumphant tour of the Yakima Valley. . . the McSon Trio. . . Alright, they'll be back here same time next week. Hope to see you then.

The audience whoops it up. As the Trio exits the stage, JACK LAUDERDALE, beautifully dressed, black, 40s, approaches Ray.

JACK
Hey baby, you sound more like Nat than the King himself. What's your name. . . ?

RAY
Ray Robinson.

In the background, Marlene sees Jack put his arm around

Ray. She zeroes in on them. . . .

JACK
Well, Ray Robinson, I'm Jack Lauderdale of Swingtime records. . . how 'bout us makin' a record together?

RAY
Hell yeah!

MARLENE *(knifing in)*
Can I help you?

JACK
I don't think so, Cool Breeze an' I are talkin' business here.

MARLENE
Then you need to talk to me. I'm his manager.

JACK
Sure, if that's the way it's blowin'. . . I'm Jack Lauderdale, of Swingtime Records.

Gossie cruises up as Marlene shakes Jack's hand.

MARLENE
I'm Marlene Andres.

Gossie offers his hand

GOSSIE
Gossie McKee. . .

Jack shakes it.

MARLENE *(turning Ray away)*
Great set, baby. We're gonna talk to Mr. Lauderdale here. . . . Come on, Jack. . . I'm buyin'.

Marlene herds Jack away from Ray. Ray's disoriented for a moment, trying to follow the sound of their footsteps in the cacophony of the club.

GOSSIE
You're doing fabulous, baby.

If you were to take the music out of this movie and only deal with Ray's personal life and his business success, it would still be a very strong story. His ability to overcome his background, his poverty, racism, the death of his young brother, going blind and being orphaned at a young age, all these elements present a really strong message about overcoming obstacles and succeeding in the real world. . . . Ray Charles was not a perfect human being but yet he managed to work through his personal demons and shortcomings. He was an extremely strong character and he had an incredibly magnetic personality. He could be a tough businessman, but he was one of the warmest, most charming people you would ever want to meet.

—Stuart Benjamin, producer

RAY
Let's talk about the record. . .

GOSSIE
Let Marlene handle that. Have Oberon order you a cab.

Marlene disappears into the crowd with Jack and Gossie. Ray stands there, listening for her voice. . . but all he hears is a chaos of laughter and clinking glasses. He's steaming now, humiliated. Suddenly, he feels a tug at his sleeve:

OBERON
Hey, Daddy-o. . . I got some gage fresh off the boat. . . clean an' seedless.

RAY *(simmering)*
Is that how it is, huh? You keep me high while they talk the business.

That stings Oberon.

OBERON
I ain't the one playin' you, man.

Oberon turns away, hurt. . . leaving Ray stranded in the crowd, alone with his frustration. His body shakes with anxiety.

RAY
Oberon. . . !

Oberon stops, turns to him. . .

EXT. THE ROCKING CHAIR CLUB–RAINY NIGHT–1949
Oberon and Ray huddle under an awning smoking a joint as rain pours down. Patrons run through the rain to their cars.

OBERON *(taking a toke)*
What if God was a dwarf. . . ?

Ray laughs and takes a hit. He gives it back to Oberon.

RAY
How 'bout a black dwarf? *(suddenly serious)* You ever get. . . mad at God?

Oberon ponders his question a moment. . . .

OBERON
Yeah. . . sometimes when I'm drunk: "Why'd you do this to me?!"

RAY
And what's he say?

OBERON
Says he'll get back to me later. *(off Ray's laughter)* I get mad at people. I asked Marlene for a raise the other day. Know what she said? I should be grateful I ain't back in the circus, gettin' out of a car with ten other midgets. *(a sad laugh)* Bitch knew just how to shut me up. . . threatenin' to take away my bacon. 'Cause you know, man, when I'm up on that stage with a mike in my hand and the lights on my face. . . ain't nobody bigger than me. Nobody, baby.

RAY *(beat)*
Yeah. . . when I play they just shut up and listen. Nobody lookin' down on me. . . no bad dreams. I'm home free.

A moment of silent recognition between them. Then. . .

OBERON
Marlene and Gossie are the ones runnin' a game on you, Ray. . .

Ray stiffens, listening intently.

OBERON *(cont'd)*
They sliced up the pie the first night you played. . . 35 percent off the top. . . plus Gossie's double-scale as the leader.

RAY
What!? If anybody's a damn leader, it's me!

Ray rises to his feet, accidentally knocks over a trash can. He's seething now. . .

RAY *(cont'd)*
You know what? To hell with those bo' humps! I'm goin' out on my own.

Oberon looks up at him sadly, a bittersweet smile.

OBERON
Who's got the contacts, Ray? Who's gonna book your gigs. . . ? *(beat)* Marlene's got you locked up, and she ain't gonna give up her golden goose.

A woman, singing to herself, passes.

WOMAN
Ray Robinson, you're fantastic.

OBERON *(sly smile)*
Gimme some skin. . .

Ray puts out his big paw and Oberon slides his little hand across it, depositing Jack Lauderdale's business card.

RAY
What's that?

OBERON
Jack's card. I got his number at the hotel. Let's call him. . .

RAY
The record cat.

INT. MARLENE'S APARTMENT–A DARK KITCHEN–NIGHT–1949

The gas burner is the only illumination as Ray fries chicken. . . and Quincy lounges at the kitchen table, cradling his trumpet like a baby.

QUINCY (V.O.)
6-9, let me turn on some lights.

RAY *(beat)*
Use the dark, 7-0. . . to find yourself a new reality.

QUINCY
Mr. B's arranger, Jimmy Valentine, can get four trumpets and four 'bones playin' eight-part harmony. . . that's another reality to me.

RAY
Simple 7-0. . . just a B flat C seven-scale it up, with a triplet off the back end.

Q blows eight quick blasts and the lights suddenly switch on. Marlene barges in with Gossie.

MARLENE
Ray, what did I tell you about cooking in the dark?

RAY
Think about it, what do I need a light for?

Marlene hears the edge in his voice. . . measures him a moment.

GOSSIE (crossing into dining room)
I need some plates.

MARLENE
Well. . . you shouldn't be cookin', anyways. We brought you take-out from Oscar's.

RAY (tosses Quincy a piece)
You should get your money back. We got fried chicken. Try that Q.

Quincy's a bit dubious, but bites into a leg, then smiles.

QUINCY
This is good.

Ray offers Marlene a piece.

MARLENE
No thank you. . .

RAY (turning to Marlene)
What'd Mr. Lauderdale have to say. . . ?

Ray's abruptness unsettles Marlene.

MARLENE (shrugs)
I clocked him out the gate, Ray. . . the man's a two-bit hustler.

GOSSIE
Only hit Swingtime ever had was "Open the Door, Richard". . . a joke record.

RAY
What about 'im wantin' to record me?

MARLENE
Oh, he'll record ya. . . if we pay the freight.

RAY (regarding her)
Scratch a liar. . . find a thief.

MARLENE
What's that suppose to mean. . . ?

RAY
This. . . (takes out a wad of money) I talked to Jack Lauderdale tonight and he gave me 500 bucks—advance on my record. He also said he'd put me

on the road with Lowell Fulson and pay me three times what you been payin' me.

MARLENE
That's a lie!

GOSSIE
John, Jim whatever his name is ain't gonna put no blind man on the road! You need watchin' out for, Ray. They ain't got time for that like we do.

RAY
Is that what you been doin' Gossie, watchin' out for me? Is that why you get paid double what I do?

GOSSIE *(beat)*
Who told you that. . . ?

RAY
It's true, ain't it? You an' Marlene been gamin' me since I got here.

MARLENE
Ray, baby, listen.

RAY
Ain't gotta listen.

GOSSIE
I been meaning to talk to you about that.

RAY
Why ain't you talking?

GOSSIE
Ray. . . don't be doin' nothin' stupid.

RAY *(bitterly)*
I may be blind. . . but I ain't stupid. *(beat)* Q, get my bag from upstairs.

QUINCY
What?

RAY
Get it!

MARLENE
Gossie, you need to fix this!

Ad libs as they walk to front door.

EXT. MARLENE'S HOUSE–NIGHT–CONTINUOUS–1949
Quincy leads Ray out into the night. . . Marlene pursuing them, Gossie following her.

MARLENE
You're makin' a big mistake, 'Bama, that clown's spoutin' promises he can't keep, you're a fool to follow 'im.

GOSSIE
Why don't we work out a new deal? Whatever you want.

RAY
The deal is, you can lay the pipe, man.

Ad libs as they scramble down the steps, Q looks at Ray, amazed.

QUINCY
Ray. . . I've never seen you like that.

RAY *(shrugs)*
That wasn't nothin', baby. . .

GOSSIE
Take your blind porch monkey ass off.

MARLENE
Ray, please come back.

GOSSIE *(giving him the finger)*
I've got something for you, in Braille. *(continues)* Don't come crawling back to me when you fall on your ass.

MARLENE
Gossie, that's enough.

FLASH BACK TO:

ARETHA ROBINSON

Ray Charles grew up in a tiny, ultra poor enclave near the Georgia/Florida border. This was the segregated South and blacks had few, if any, rights. Ray and his little brother, George, hardly knew their father (he had three families.) However, his mother was the rock of his existence. By all accounts she was an incredible woman.

Her name was Aretha Robinson and even though she was young, poor, and uneducated, she worked hard to raise her two boys by taking in laundry. She suffered from poor health but she had a very fierce, independent spirit that she passed on to her sons.

When Ray talked about his mother, it was clear that she was the most important person in his life and the one to whom he gave credit for making him the person he became. He told me sincerely that throughout his life, he spoke to his mother every day and I created special moments in the film to reflect these "dreams." Obviously, casting Aretha was a challenge of major proportions but fortune shone on us in the form of a young actress named Sharon Warren.

Sharon had no professional experience in film or TV, but she possessed a huge, burning talent that matched Aretha's intensity. When I showed Jamie the videotape we'd made of Sharon, he was overwhelmed. She was the only actress we interviewed.

After I cut the movie together, I took it to RC's office to play it for him. The first character he wanted to hear was his mother and after listening to Sharon's performance, he smiled and said, "Taylor, I'm very happy, I'm very pleased."

Nothing could mean more to me than that.

—Taylor Hackford

EXT. EULA'S YARD–JELLYROLL, FLORIDA–DAY–1935
Two little black boys run through a maze of white sheets, hanging from clotheslines. They're YOUNG RAY, 5—his eyes normal—and GEORGE, 4, Ray's younger brother.

Suddenly, a sheet is ripped down, falling onto the red clay dirt. Another is ripped off, then another hits the dirt revealing ARETHA ROBINSON—the woman who appeared in Ray's two previous Dream Sequences—skinny, bone-tired, and hopping mad. The boys stare in shock at their mother.

EULA—a massive black woman in her 40s—storms up to little Aretha ready to do battle.

> EULA
> Aretha Robinson, have you lost your mind?

> ARETHA
> Eula Banks, you promised to split every wash basket
> with me, fair an' square!

> EULA
> An' I did!

> ARETHA
> Hell you did! You charged 'em white folks one thing,
> an' paid me 'nother!

> EULA
> Who's gonna wash these?!

> ARETHA
> You can! Now pay me my money!

For a moment, big Eula thinks about crushing this little bird, but Aretha steps forward fiercely, holding out her hand. Eula backs down. . . takes a change purse from her bosom.

> EULA
> I'm gonna give you two little dollars. . . but don't 'spect
> no more work from me.

> ARETHA
> I got all I need outta you.

Storyboard artist Raymond Prado drew this image of Aretha, Ray's mother, long before Sharon Warren (who looks remarkably like this drawings) was cast in the role.

Aretha snatches her money and marches off.

ARETHA (cont'd)
Ray, George. . . come on.

Young Ray and George have to run to keep up with their angry mother.

ARETHA (cont'd) (still steaming)
Y'all gotta learn to read an' write real good, so you never have to work for people like that. . . scratch a liar, find a thief, understand?

YOUNG RAY
Yessum, Mama.

Off Young Ray's clear, seeing eyes as he soaks up his mother's words. . .

DISSOLVE BACK TO:

MONTAGE OF LOS ANGELES, 1950—DAY
City Hall, Venice Beach, Paramount, Central Avenue. . .

JACK (V.O.)
L.A.'s where it's at, Ray. A town where the Negro can spread his wings.

INT. THE CLUB ALABAMA–NIGHT–1950
Ray, transformed by a totally new wardrobe, haircut, and sunglasses, holds Jack's elbow as a maitre d' leads them through the plushest of L.A.'s black clubs. (Ad libs as Jack and Ray enter to include):

JACK
We're celebrating tonight. . . champagne! Smell that Ray, it's the smell of success. Take three steps into your new world baby. . .

As they walk down the steps. . .

JACK (cont'd)
How do the new rags feel?

RAY
Like a cool breeze.

JACK
There you go baby, you gotta present your best face to the world.

Onstage, Art Tatum performs.

RAY *(listening)*
Oh, man I know my ears aren't playin' tricks on me. . . is that Art Tatum?

JACK
Sure is, wanna meet him?

RAY *(stammers, intimidated)*
I. . . I couldn't. . . he's the most.

JACK
So are you, Ray. So are you. . . *(to photographer)* Get this picture, darlin' *(she takes a picture)* Everybody's here tonight. At the back bar, that's Scatman Crothers *(a whisper)* And behind him, Lillian Randolph.

RAY *(star struck)*
Madame McQueen on *Amos 'n Andy*?!

JACK
You know, we've gotta do something about your name. Sugar Ray's already got the Robinson franchise sewn up. How 'bout we go with your middle name, call you *Ray Charles?*

RAY *(laughs)*
I don't care what you call me as long as my name is on the record.

LOWELL (V.O.)
What's the haps, Jack? Give me some skin.

LOWELL FULSON, a flamboyant black band leader, 40s, leans in.

JACK
Hey. . . Lowell Fulson, I want you to meet Ray. . . Charles.

CLOTHES THAT MAKE THE MAN

Ray moves so swiftly that at times I thought it was an action biopic. Ray is in the studio, he is at home, he is on stage. We shot about ten nightclub scenes and eight big auditorium performances. Almost every one of the scenes takes place in a different year so I had to show the passage of time in costumes.

Jamie had more than 100 wardrobe changes. We had initial fittings where I explained what we were doing. After that, we would just give him his clothes and he would always be happy with them.

In the beginning of the movie, Ray wears the same clothes over and over again. For the Seattle scenes, set in 1947, we put him in an old 1930s suit, pants up to here, suspenders, and a bow tie. I wanted him to look like someone gave him the clothes and he had had them for years.

At the end of the Seattle sequence, Ray starts to gain respect for his music and we see a gradual change in his clothing. By the time Jeff enters the picture, all of Ray's clothes are impeccable. We had Jamie's clothes tailor-made for him because that is how Ray Charles always dressed.

—SHAREN DAVIS, COSTUME DESIGNER

LOWELL *(shaking Ray's hand)*
Ray Charles. . . the "blind sensation."

JACK
Damn. . . I'll have to put that on the album cover.

RAY
He's the sensation. . . I love your music, Mr. Fulson.

LOWELL *(to Jack)*
The man's got taste.

JACK
The "man" has never been on the road, Lowell. . . so take care of him.

LOWELL
Like my own brother.

Lowell gestures silently to Jack. . . guiding his attention to two fine, young women at the bar.

JACK *(to Ray)*
Ray, I'll be right back. . .

Lowell and Jack rise in unison, sauntering up to the women. Ray is left alone, disoriented for a moment by the chaos of the club. But then, he focuses on the music. . . on Art Tatum. *Slowly, the other sounds in the room begin to diminish. We're HEARING what Ray hears as he filters out the club's noise. . . and zeroes in on Art's Tatum's brilliance.* In a moment, Ray is gently rocking. . . lost in the music.

FLASHBACK TO:

EXT. JELLYROLL, FLORIDA–DAY–1935
Young Ray, his eyes clear and seeing, runs with little brother George through Jellyroll, a dirt-poor colored enclave in northern Florida, replete with tin-roofed cabins. Suddenly, Ray stops short, looking toward the general store. . . caught by the music playing inside.

GEORGE
Don't you be going in that Red Wing. . . you heard what Mama said.

YOUNG RAY
You go on. . . don't tell Mama nothin' *(running toward the music)* Get outta here.

Ray runs into the Red Wing.

INT. GENERAL STORE–DAY–1935
Ray enters and slips past a few people chatting with the two clerks. He peeks over the counter. . . and into the adjoining Red Wing Cafe, where a man sits playing the piano.

INT. THE RED WING CAFE–DAY–1935
CLOSE UP: delicate fingers pound out a mean boogie-woogie; drop focus to young Ray slipping into the room.

The place is empty. . . except for MR. PIT, 40s, slicked hair, playing an old upright piano. Ray watches in awe. Finally, Mr. Pit notices him.

MR. PIT
Hey, boy. . . who let you in?

Ray starts to retreat. . .

MR. PIT *(cont'd)*
You're 'Retha's son, ain't ya?

YOUNG RAY *(nods)*
Yes, sir, Ray Charles Robinson.

MR. PIT
Yeah. . . I seen you sneakin' 'round here before. Ya like the piana? *(off Ray's nod)* Ya know, this here box can talk. . .

He kicks the sound board, then pounds out chords that make the piano shriek in pain. Ray laughs.

MR. PIT *(cont'd)*
Wanna learn how to play?

In the Deep South, bottles were hung from trees to capture evil spirits. This tradition originated in Africa and was used by the filmmakers for authenticity of the time and place where Ray Charles grew up.

BOTTLE TREE

For the "Jellyroll" locations, we used an old sharecroppers plantation that still had most of the out buildings intact. We brought in about sixty tons of red dirt from Georgia for the roads and grounds, built a new "Robinson home" (with fly walls and false ceilings) and made stables, pig pens, gardens, and cemeteries. We also put in a "bottle tree" in one of the yards, which was used quite a lot for transitions in the film. I had seen one of these in Mississippi, a few years earlier and it was intriguing. There are many versions about their African/West-Indies origin. Some say they hold the souls of the white plantation masters, others that they keep the bad spirits or "ju-ju" away.

—Stephen Altman, production designer

Ray just stands there. . . intimidated yet filled with desire.

MR. PIT (cont'd)
C'mere, son. . .
(plays three notes) Can you do that?

Ray watches very carefully, then plays the three notes.

MR. PIT (cont'd)
Good. Now do it faster.

Ray picks up the pace and Mr. Pit starts to accompany him. Gaining confidence, Ray bangs out his three notes, and Mr. Pit explodes, incorporating Ray's notes into a wild boogie-woogie. Ray's in ecstasy. . . his first religious experience.

CUT BACK TO:

EXT. COUNTRY ROAD–DAY–1950
Lowell Fulson's tour bus passes by a sign OKLAHOMA HWY 152.

WILBUR (V.O.)
Each club we hit, it'll be your responsibility to rehearse the band.

INT. LOWELL FULSON'S TOUR BUS–MOVING–DAY–1950
The road manager, WILBUR J. BRASSFIELD—40s, black— stands in the aisle, lecturing Ray. In the background, the other band members are gambling, shooting craps.

WILBUR
They're lazy-ass bastards, so don't let 'em slough off.

Lowell Fulson snores in the front seat, oblivious.

WILBUR (cont'd)
You gotta be dressed and ready to open the show. Lowell takes a nap before he goes on, so you do your thing till he feels like comin' out. Then, when Lowell's playin', you keep the band sharp.

RAY
One thing. . . ?

WILBUR
What?

RAY
Did Jack tell you, I wanna be paid in singles?

WILBUR
Jes do your job. . . you'll get your money.

Wilbur leans toward JEFF BROWN, late 20s, the bus driver.

WILBUR (CONT'D)
What was that?

JEFF
I don't know. I didn't hear nothin'.

WILBUR
That ping in the engine.

JEFF (shrugs)
Had it tuned 'fore we left.

WILBUR (suddenly angry)
Told you not to be spendin' money without tellin' me!

JEFF (locking eyes with Wilbur)
I did the work myself.

Like most bullies, Wilbur's a coward. . . but he covers his retreat by turning his anger on the band.

WILBUR (to the musicians)
Alright, you clowns, break up that game. . . and that means you, Fathead!

DAVID "FATHEAD" NEWMAN, 30s, black, mutters something under his breath and the other band members all crack up.

EXT. THE HALF MOON (MEMPHIS)–NIGHT–1950
A NEON SIGN flashes above a ramshackle nightclub.

INT. THE HALF MOON–NIGHT–1950
Working men and women crowd into this tiny club listening to LOWELL FULSON perform "Rock This House," but the band

is road-weary, sluggish. . . uninspired. Ray tries to spike up the tempo but he can't get the musicians' attention. He fumes. . .

DISSOLVE TO:

INT. THE HALF MOON–DAY–1950
Sunlight blasts through an open door behind the stage revealing this to be a real dump. The band members are sleepy and pissed off that Ray's called a morning rehearsal. Jeff hustles Jimmy in.

JEFF
You're forty-five minutes late.

JIMMY (bass)
Don't be pushin' me. I ain't rehearsin' this early for nobody.

RAY
You wanna get some sleep, you need to start doin' your job. Your ass was draggin' last night, an' I ain't gonna stand for it. Lowell Fulson wants to fire me, fine. . . but as long as I'm in charge of this band, we're gonna play tight. (beat) Now pay attention. . . the saxophone starts on the fourth beat with an eighth-note triplet. Then, B flat, C, D, an' hold the D over the bar. . . got it?

Fathead nods, impressed.

RAY (cont'd)
Drummer, you watch my right foot an' shoulder for the cue. Okay, 1,2,3,4.

They attack their new charts, noticeably tighter.

MATCH CUT TO:

INT. THE HALF MOON–NIGHT–1950
On stage, Lowell Fulson performs "Rock This House" to a standing-room-only crowd. Ray and the band are so hot, Lowell can barely keep up. . .

LOWELL
Slow down. . .

DISSOLVE TO:

INT. THE HALF MOON–NIGHT–LATER–1950–
MUSIC CONTINUES
The musicians pack up their instruments, chatting with some
bad girls. At the piano, Ray listens to their sexual banter.

> **FATHEAD**
> But dig. . . what I really want to know is if any of
> you fine young ladies know where we can get us
> a steak this time a night?

> **FAST GIRL**
> You mean somethin' big, thick, and juicy?

The musicians sing out an affirmative chorus.

> **RAY** (*smiling, friendly*)
> Hey, where you cats goin'?

The band members look at one another.

> **JIMMY** (*bass*) (*whispers to Fathead*)
> I ain't baby-sittin' no blind cat.

> **FATHEAD** (*subdued*)
> Sorry, Ray. . . law says six to a cab. Next time,
> I promise, baby.

The musicians and the girls scamper off together, joking and
laughing. Silence. Ray is completely alone in the club. . . . A
series of TIME DISSOLVES extends his isolation. . . until the
silence is deafening. Finally, Ray picks out a mournful blues
melody on the piano. . . which SEGUES TO Lowell Fulson's
"Everyday I Have the Blues."

EXT. NEON SIGN–THE SANDPIPER CLUB–NIGHT–1950

INT. THE SANDPIPER CLUB–NIGHT–1950
Lowell and the band perform "Everyday" to a packed house.

**INT. OTHER CLUB #1 (CROOKED ACE) & OTHER CLUB #2
(SATURN BAR)–NIGHT–MUSIC CONTINUES**

**EXT. LOWELL'S BUS ON COUNTRY ROAD–DAY–
MUSIC CONTINUES**

I feel sometimes like I'm lost in a dark forest with huge trees. And behind every tree there are ghosts.

—Ray Charles, Michael Lydon, *Ray Charles*, 1998

INT. LOWELL'S BUS–DAY–1950–(MUSIC CONTINUES)
Jeff drives as the band gamble and talk. Ray sits by himself, wide awake. . . isolated and alone.

INT. THE CLUB ALABAMA–DAY–1950 (MUSIC CONTINUES)
It's payday and Wilbur counts out cash across the bar to the band members. He's agile and fast, like a card shark. He slips a dollar off Fathead's pay.

> **WILBUR**
> That's for bein' late to the bus.

> **FATHEAD**
> Wilbur, you lowdown. . .

> **WILBUR**
> You better move on.

As Ray steps up Wilbur looks at him with contempt.

> **WILBUR** *(cont'd)*
> Mister One Dollar Bill.

Ray keeps his cool. Wilbur picks up a stack of ones and starts counting.

> CUT TO FLASHBACK:

INT. EMPTY COUNTRY WESTERN BAR–DAY–1947
Close-up: white hands counting out one dollar bills.

> **BILLY RAY** (V.O.)
> Five, ten, fifteen, twenty. . .

He's dealing them out like fives, not ones. Suddenly, another white hand ENTERS FRAME, grabbing Billy Ray's wrist.

> **TIL** (V.O.)
> You wanna start again?

Til holds Billy Ray in a vice-like grip. Ray stands there, trying to figure out what's going on.

> **BILLY RAY** *(in pain)*
> Come on Til, I'm givin' this boy what he's due!

> **TIL**
> Yeah? Well, you better start givin' 'im what he's worth.

Billy Ray stares up at Til with hatred, but Til won't flinch. Finally, Billy Ray begins to count for real.

> **WILBUR** (V.O.)
> . . . 24, 25, 26, 27. . .

> CUT BACK TO:

INT. CLUB ALABAMA–DAY–1950–MUSIC CONTINUES
Frustrated, Wilbur stops counting the singles for Ray.

> **WILBUR**
> I ain't YOUR damn seein' eye dog. . .

He slaps the money down and storms off. Ray patiently counts out the rest.

EXT. HIGHWAYS–DAY–1950–MUSIC CONTINUES
A montage of highway signs: Texas Hwy 180. . . Louisiana I-25. . . Mississippi 61. . . Ohio Tollway.

INT. THE ANOTHER CLUB–BACKSTAGE–NIGHT–1950
Ray bangs on the bathroom door.

> **RAY**
> Fathead, open the door, it's Ray. I gotta take a leak.

Fathead opens the door a crack.

> **JIMMY** (bass) (V.O.)
> What you doin' man? Close the door.

> **FATHEAD** (beat)
> Ray. . . we're gonna be awhile. Use the women's can. It's over there on the right.

Humiliated, Ray starts to walk away, but trips over something and falls down onto:

A wet floor. Ray reaches out. . . And feels the cold, dead leg of the little black boy. He recoils with a muted cry. . .

Fathead sticks his head out of the bathroom.

> **FATHEAD** (cont'd)
> You okay, Ray?

> **RAY** (quickly getting up)
> 'S nothin'. I slipped on the wet. . . busted pipe or something, water everywhere.

Fathead looks down skeptically. . . the floor is bone dry.

    FATHEAD
Go ahead, quit playing now.

                    FADE TO BLACK:

EXT. TENNESSEE HIGHWAY–DAY–1950
MOVING P.O.V. over Jeff's shoulder of a TENNESSEE HWY #49 sign, as we streak past.

INT. LOWELL'S TOUR BUS–DAY–1950–MUSIC CONTINUES
The musicians party and gamble in the back of the bus. Ray sits behind Jeff. . . alone in the crowd. It's all he can do to keep from crying. Jeff glances into the rearview mirror.

    JEFF
So. . . where you from, Ray?

Ray just sits there a moment.

    RAY
North Florida.

    JEFF
North Florida boy? Your people still down there?

    RAY
No. . .

    JEFF
Pardon me for askin'. . . but how do ya get around so good without a cane or a dog?

    RAY *(an edge)*
How do you get around without a cane or a dog?

    JEFF *(gently)*
Sorry. . . didn't mean to pry.

Ray can hear the concern in Jeff's voice. Slowly, he starts to tap his shoe against a metal post. Jeff looks up.

    RAY
My ears gotta be my eyes, man. . .

Ray stamps his foot on the rubber mat, kicks the bottom of the seat. . . then taps the post again.

    RAY *(cont'd)*
Everythin' sounds different. . . see? I wear hard-soled shoes so I can hear the echo of my footsteps off the walls. Then, when I pass an open doorway. . . the sound changes.

    JEFF
That's cool. . .

    RAY *(secretly pleased)*
Yeah, well. . . you use what ya got.

    JEFF
How long it take ya to learn that?

    RAY
You learn pretty fast. . . if you want to get around on your own.

Jeff can hear the weariness in his voice.

    JEFF
Yeah. . . durin' the war, there was a whole lot I had to learn up fast. . . or I wouldn't be here. *(shakes his head)* Seein' that much death ain't natural.

    RAY *(quietly)*
Seein' death. . . ain't natural

Ray leans his head against the window and goes silent.

                    FADE TO BLACK:

EXT. ROBINSON HOME/BACK YARD–DAY–1935–RAY'S FLASHBACK
Young Ray and George are playing in the street. George chases Ray.

    ARETHA
Get away from that still. You know better than that. Get away from around the fire. You need to get cleaned up for dinner. . .

Aretha lugs her empty basket back to the house.

INSIDE HOUSE
Aretha gathers more clothes.

> **ARETHA** *(cont'd)*
> I'm cooking some field peas, rice, and I got some
> of that smothered corn left, and if you're real good,
> two pieces of peach cobbler.

OUTSIDE
The boys are playing tag.

> **GEORGE**
> I got you! I got you!

> **YOUNG RAY** *(laughing)*
> No, you didn't! You missed!

George stops in his tracks, frustrated and exhausted.

> **GEORGE**
> Stop cheatin', Ray!

> **YOUNG RAY**
> Okay, okay. . . you got me. . . *(taps George back)* . . .
> but I got you back!

With that, Young Ray is off and running. George just looks
at him.

> **GEORGE** *(to himself)*
> I ain't playin' no mo'. . . .

George climbs up the sawhorses that support the rinse tub.

> **GEORGE** *(cont'd)*
> Come and get me, Ray. Play with me, Ray.

> **YOUNG RAY**
> Better get down 'fore Mama sees ya.

> **GEORGE**
> Look, I'm a giant!

George scoffs at Young Ray, prancing around the tub.
Suddenly, he loses his balance and tumbles head first into
the water. George's ass is in the air, his feet kicking and
splashing. . . a comic sight and Young Ray falls down, laughing.

Aretha Robinson had two children, Ray, her first born, and George, who was a year younger. According to Ray, George was the smarter brother but of course, Ray felt a huge amount of guilt about George's tragic death which had all the trappings of a Greek tragedy. At the age of five, little Ray watched his four-year-old brother drown in a washtub. Ray laughed when George first slipped and fell into the tub, he thought it was funny but then, as he described it to me, he became paralyzed and just stood there watching his brother drown before his eyes.

Nine months after George died, Ray started losing his sight; by the age of seven, he was completely blind. While Ray didn't have a doctor to diagnose his condition back then, he probably had juvenile glaucoma. However he didn't seem to experience any symptoms before the tragedy of his brother's death. Clearly, Ray blamed himself for his brother's freak accident and suffered from what is called the guilt of the surviving sibling. If you have a brother or sister who dies, you tend to have an intense need to achieve and to prove that God was right in choosing you to be the survivor. You begin living and accomplishing for two.

There are many famous people, Elvis Presley and Richard Nixon for example, who lost their siblings at a young age.

Over the course of his life RC was haunted by this horrible vision of George's death. The psychological ramifications are fascinating and in the film we decided to use this tragedy as a seminal event in Ray's life. Clearly, Ray Charles was an immense talent. But the question remains: Would his talent have been as finely tuned if he had not gone blind in the way he did?

—Taylor Hackford

YOUNG RAY
Some giant! Look at you. . . !

George's legs flail frantically now, but Ray is laughing too hard to notice.

Finally, George stops moving. . . and Ray stops laughing. He rises slowly. . . confused, afraid.

RAY
George stop! This ain't funny. I ain't playin' that game.

Aretha steps outside with another basketful of clothes.

ARETHA
Didn't I tell you to come in the house?

She SEES Ray standing there, paralyzed. . . staring at the rinse tub. Aretha starts to call out to him. . . when she spots George, face down in the water.

ARETHA *(cont'd)*
Dear God. . . no!

Aretha drops her basket, dashes to the tub. She pulls George out. . . and desperately tries to shake the water from his lungs. Neighbors hearing Aretha's cries come running.

ARETHA *(cont'd)*
Breathe, baby. . . breathe for Mama!

Aretha lifts George's head. . . and it drops lifelessly to his chest. She slumps to the ground, weeping over the body of her little son. SUDDENLY, she turns and grabs Ray, shaking him hard.

ARETHA *(cont'd)*
Why didn't you do somethin'?! Why didn't you come an' get me. . . ?!

Ray is devastated. . . he can't answer her. The neighbors form a circle around them. Aretha picks up George's lifeless body and carries him through the crowd into the house. Ray just stands there in shock, staring into the water. . .

FADE TO BLACK:

INT. LOWELL'S TOUR BUS–DAY–1950
Ray, tortured by the memory, is rocked as the bus stops.

EXT. MERCEDES HOUSE–DAY

WILBUR (V.O.)
Food and piss stop.

Wilbur opens the door to the bus and steps out.

WILBUR *(cont'd)*
Food's hot. . . y'all got 45 minutes!

Lowell hears the word *food* and rushes past Wilbur, scurrying down the steps.

LOWELL
I could eat a horse.

The band members follow him, streaming toward a modest house in a black neighborhood.

Ray waits at the top of the stairs. . . always the last to go. Fathead and Jimmy the bass player swagger down the steps.

FATHEAD
Wilbur, we need more'n 45 minutes.

WILBUR
Not to eat you don't. If ya' got "other business," better choose. . . 'cause this bus is rollin' on time.

JIMMY *(Bass) (whispers to Fathead)*
Come on. . . Mercedes gotta washroom in the back.

WILBUR *(to Ray)*
You can smell it.

Ray's ears perk up. . . they're at it again. He turns to Jeff.

RAY
Can you help me inside, man. . . ?

JEFF
Sure thing.

INT. MERCEDES' HOUSE–KITCHEN–DAY
A black woman, MERCEDES, sets out steaming bowls of country cooking for the hungry musicians. Ray and Jeff enter.

JEFF
Miss Mercedes, where's the can at?

Ad libs continue. Jeff leads Ray into the hallway.

> What I never understood to this day, to this very day, was how white people could have black people cook for them, make their meals, but wouldn't let them sit at the table with them. How can you dislike someone so much and have them cook for you? Shoot, if I don't like someone you ain't cooking nothing for me, ever.
>
> —Ray Charles

JEFF *(cont'd)*
There's a dresser on the right-hand side.

Guiding Ray down the hall.

JEFF *(cont'd)*
It's right in front of you.

RAY
Thanks, man. I got it from here.

JEFF
Want me to fix you plate?

RAY
I'm good.

JEFF
You sure?

RAY
I'm Okay.

Jeff returns to the dining room.

RAY *(cont'd)*
Jeff?

Assured that Jeff is gone, Ray slips down the hall.

CUT TO:

INT. MERCEDES' HOUSE–LAUNDRY ROOM–DAY–1950
Close-up: A LEATHER BELT is tightened around a bicep. Jimmy the bass player is tying-off as Fathead cooks a spoon of heroin. Suddenly, Ray pushes his way into the room.

JIMMY *(bass)*
Hey, man! The can's down the hall.

RAY
I know. What y'all doin'. . . ?

JIMMY *(bass)*
Do yourself a favor an' leave.

RAY
I'll leave when I'm ready. . . c'mon Fathead, I want in.

FATHEAD
Ray, this ain't no weed, an' we ain't snortin' no Bitch. This is BOY—an' Boy'll make your ass null 'n void—so get on outta here.

RAY
Null 'n void? Just like my life, baby. I'll be right at home.

JIMMY *(bass)*
I ain't gonna wait all night. It's his funeral, man.

FATHEAD *(takes Ray's arm)*
C'mon, let's get somethin' to eat.

RAY *(pulling away)*
I ain't leavin' till I get a taste.

FATHEAD
I ain't havin' nothin' to do with this. I warned ya, Ray. . .

Fathead exits. Ray inhales the odor of cooked heroin.

RAY
Yeah. I been warned. . .

JIMMY
Sit down, man. I'm gonna take you on a little trip, but it'll cost you.

Ray offers him some money.

RAY
Will this do?

JIMMY
It'll do.

CUT TO:

INT. MERCEDES' HOUSE–LAUNDRY ROOM–DAY–1950
Extreme close-up: fingers squeeze an eye dropper with a needle attached, sucking liquid heroin through a piece of cotton that's soaking in a spoon.

INT. MERCEDES' HOUSE–LAUNDRY ROOM–DAY–1950
Ray's face fills with anticipation.

> **JIMMY** *(bass)* **(V.O.)**
> You're gonna feel a little pinch.

INT. ROBINSON HOME–NIGHT–1935–THIRD ARETHA DREAM
Aretha stands, silhouetted in the doorway of her farmhouse. She turns to camera. . . a look of pity and anger on her face.

> **ARETHA**
> I ain't givin' up on you, boy.

Aretha's image is slowly consumed by blackness.

INT. MERCEDES' HOUSE–LAUNDRY ROOM–DAY–1950
Ray hesitates a moment, as if hearing her. Then. . .

> **RAY**
> Go ahead.

He winces as the needle pierces his skin. As the dope takes over, Ray begins to breathe through his mouth.

> **JIMMY** *(bass)*
> Feel it, baby?

> **RAY**
> Yeah, I feel it.

> **JIMMY** *(bass)*
> Take the ride. It's better 'n sex.

> **RAY**
> Ain't nothin' better 'n sex.

Ray lays his head lazily against the wall, tripping. We hear the haunting wail of GOSPEL VOICES rising.

EXT. FRONT PORCH–DAY–1935
Ray sitting on the porch on a windy day. He is shaking a toy, listening. He wipes his heavily tearing eyes. Aretha goes into the house.

> **ARETHA**
> C'mon in for dinner, Ray. Stop rubbing those eyes. C'mon, boy.

Ray stares out again, then follows her in.

EXT. FRONT PORCH–DAY–1935
It is a rainy day. Aretha is peeling vegetables. Ray sits beating his drum. Aretha gets up.

> **ARETHA**
> Come in, baby, before you get a cold.

FLASHBACK TO:

EXT. NEW SHILOH BAPTIST CHURCH–DAY–1935
A tiny church in need of paint, surrounded by dense greenery.

INT. NEW SHILOH BAPTIST CHURCH–DAY–1935
A little casket rests on the altar. Aretha sits in the front row, sobbing. . . Young Ray and Mr. Pit at her side.

The citizens of Jellyroll sing out their anguish, trying to exorcise Aretha's pain. Mr. Pit puts his arm around Young Ray. . . but the boy is glassy eyed, still in shock. He can't even sing. Aretha cries out in anguish, falling across George's casket. . .

EXT. FRONT PORCH–DAY–1935
Ray, his eyes teary, sits on the front porch. Aretha comes out.

> **ARETHA**
> C'mon Ray let me put this salve I got from Dr. McLoud in your eyes.

> **YOUNG RAY**
> I don't like that, it stings!

> **ARETHA**
> C'mon Boy, I paid a dollar for it. I hope it works.

INT. ROBINSON HOME–DAY–1935 FLASHBACK CONTINUES
Aretha and Ray sit on the front porch. His eyes are oozing mucus.

> **ARETHA**
> Baby, come here and let me clear that mess out of your eyes. *(she gently wipes his eyes)* Ray. . . I ain't gonna beat 'round the bush. You're goin' blind. The doctors say ain't nothin' they can do, so we gotta do it ourselves.

YOUNG RAY *(starts to cry)*
Yessum. . . I know, but. . .

ARETHA *(snapping)*
Boy, stop it! Stop it, right now!

Young Ray is startled by Aretha's sharp tone.

ARETHA *(cont'd)*
We ain't got time for no tears. . . ain't nobody gonna
have pity on ya, jes 'cause you're blind. . . an' ya can't
have no pity on yourself—it'll eat you alive. Now. . .
wipe away 'em tears.

YOUNG RAY *(wiping his eyes)*
Yessum.

ARETHA
Okay. I'll show you how to do somethin' once. . . an' I'll
help you if you mess up twice. But the third time, you're
on your own. . . 'cause that's the way it is in the world.
Understand. . . ? Now get up. *(they stand up)* Remember,
you're goin' blind, but you ain't stupid. You remember
how many steps there are?

YOUNG RAY
Four. . .

ARETHA
Good. . . learn to use your memory.

She leads him forward

ARETHA *(cont'd)*
Now hold your hands out and use them as your eyes.

Ray fumbles for the front door and walks in, followed by
Aretha.

INT. ROBINSON HOME–DAY
Aretha begins to lead him around the house, touching his
hand to everything they pass.

ARETHA
I'll keep everythin' in the same place. Rockin' chair's

right here, inside the front door. . . straight ahead's
the kitchen. . .

Aretha leads Ray into the kitchen. She holds his hand out
toward the stove. Suddenly, he yanks it back.

ARETHA (CONT'D)
Stove's easy to find. . . *(beat)* . . . an' the water bucket's
over here.

She puts his hand in the water.

YOUNG RAY
Yessum.

ARETHA
I'll do it again, then you show me.

FADE TO BLACK:

A 45RPM RECORD SPINNING INTO FRAME–1951
Swingtime's "Baby Let Me Hold Your Hand" on the label. The
music fades in, segueing to. . .

EXT. EBONY LOUNGE (CLEVELAND, OHIO)–NIGHT

INT. EBONY LOUNGE (CLEVELAND, OHIO)–NIGHT–1951

WILBUR
Fool makes one record. . . an' you'd think *he* was the
star of this band.

On stage, Ray performs "Baby Let Me Hold Your Hand" to a
capacity crowd. Lowell and Wilbur watch from the wings.

LOWELL
He's got somethin'. . . ain't he?

WILBUR
His wax won't even hit the charts. *(kissing up)*
You're still the man, baby. . .

But Lowell isn't so certain. . .

DISSOLVE TO:

INT. EBONY LOUNGE–NIGHT–1951–MUSIC CONTINUES
Ray's hand slipping around a woman's wrist.

> **FATHEAD**
> Look at Ray, y'all.

As Fathead and the other musicians move their instruments,
Ray sits at the bar, flirting with a girl in a yellow dress.

> **FATHEAD** *(cont'd)*
> See that? He feels her wrist 'cause he figures that's the
> way to tell if she's good lookin' or not.

They laugh. . . until the girl walks off with Ray.

> **FATHEAD** *(cont'd)*
> See what a lil' fame does to "Null 'n Void"?

Wilbur rushes up to them.

> **WILBUR**
> Anybody seen that fine-lookin' gal in the yellow dress?

Fathead and the guys laugh in Wilbur's face.

CUT TO:

A montage OF RAY'S WOMEN —

INT. VARIOUS CLUBS–NIGHT–1951
INTERCUT: Series of shots of RAY'S HAND, feeling the slender
wrists of young women. . .

INT. VARIOUS HOTELS–NIGHT–1951
. . . with SHOTS OF HOTEL ROOM DOORS opening to reveal
each girl, ready for action. . . one time, it's two girls.

INT. VARIOUS HOTEL ROOMS–NIGHT–1951
. . . then REVERSE ANGLE ON RAY, a bed in the background,
as each girl slinks past him into his hotel room.

RIGHT: Storyboard art by Raymond Prado illustrating the
sequence of scenes depicting RC's seduction techniques.

-CUT TO: -Door opens
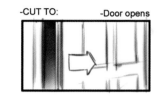

-Door closes on camera

-Revealing CU Woman

-Match cut. Door opens

- Ray Charles

-Revealing a new woman

-CU Hands shake

-CU Ray

-Wrist touch

-Wrist touch

-Ray

-Ext. hotel hallway

-Woman enters & crosses Ray

-Woman leaves Room
-Cut:

-To Hotel room bed in BG

-New Woman enters
-Cut:

-Two women exit

CUT TO:

INT. ROBINSON HOUSE–DAY–1936
Young Ray runs into the house, Aretha is just behind him.

YOUNG RAY
Mama, I'm going to get a drink of water. . .

He trips and falls.

YOUNG RAY (cont'd)
Mama, help, Mama. . .

ARETHA
I told you that rocking chair is always going to be in the same place. Now that's number two, there ain't gonna be no number three. There ain't nothin' free in this world 'cept Jesus. . .

She leads him away.

ARETHA (cont'd)
C'mon now, I'm gonna show you where everything else is again. . .

INT. CROOKED ACE–BACKSTAGE–DAY
THREE TEN-DOLLAR BILLS, TWO FIVES, AND A STACK OF ONES, LAYING ON A TABLE.

Wilbur is paying the band.

WILBUR
It's a shame, Jimmy, you're gonna piss it away right up your arm.

JIMMY
You don't tell me what to do with my money.

WILBUR (to Ray)
The one-dollar sensation!

He hands Ray his money.

RAY
You wanna keep on countin'?

Wilbur looks up at Ray from his desk.

WILBUR
What's a matter, boy. . . fifty bucks ain't enough for ya?

RAY
That ain't fifty. . . keep countin'.

WILBUR
Guess you're lookin' for charity. . . since that record of yours ain't sellin'.

WITHOUT WARNING, Ray jumps on Wilbur, knocking him to the floor. They roll around. . . punching, biting, kicking. Jeff, Fathead, and Lowell rush over to separate them.

LOWELL
What the hell's goin' on?!

WILBUR
The *Blind Sensation* here don't like the money I'm payin' 'im!

RAY
He's cheatin' me! I quit!

WILBUR
You're a lyin' son-of-a-bitch. . . .

Everyone felt like they knew Ray Charles and in a way they did, because he was embodied by his music. We were on tour and playing these tobacco barns in the South and the crowd would just be packed in to see him. The women would come up to the bandstand and yell, "Just let me touch him once!" It was like he had descended from heaven, a beloved idol and an inspiration to so many of us.

—Ahmet Ertegun, *Rolling Stone*, July 8-22, 2004

As Ray walks off, his foot kicks a chair as we:

CUT TO FLASHBACK:

INT. ROBINSON HOUSE–DAY–1936
. . . AND young Ray falls down hard, INTO FRAME.

> **YOUNG RAY**
> Mama. . . ? Where are you? I need you.

The blind boy waits a moment. . . listening for her footsteps.

Aretha watches from the kitchen. . . but she doesn't move as Ray fumbles around helplessly, trying to get his moorings.

> **YOUNG RAY** *(cont'd) (crying out)*
> Mama! Help me. . .

Aretha stands there silently, watching. . . fighting back her emotions. After a long beat, Young Ray pulls himself up. He begins to tilt his head from side to side, using his ears to AMPLIFY THE SOUNDS in the room. . . to create an aural landscape.

FATHEAD
You shouldn't be fighting someone you can't see.

WILBUR *(to Lowell)*
I just stopped runnin' 'round, tryin' to find singles for this chump!

JEFF *(counting the money)*
There's fifty dollars here, Ray.

WILBUR
See there, FOOL?!

LOWELL
Shut-up, Wilbur. Ray, from now on I'll take care of your pay myself.

RAY
No, I'm finished, Lowell. I'll talk to Jack and tell 'im to find you someone else.

LOWELL
You sure, man. . . it's cold out there.

RAY
Don't worry about me, baby, I can take care of myself.

> You have to ask yourself, "Why was I born? Was it just to die?" When you get down to the bottom line, that's the question. The important thing is to make the best of your life, to try and to contribute something. You don't gain anything by giving up.
>
> —Ray Charles, *Los Angeles Times*, February 28, 1980

INT. ROBINSON HOUSE–DAY–1936
Young Ray turns toward the KETTLE on the stove, hears its subtle HISS. He walks to the fireplace and quickly withdraws his hand.

EXT. ROBINSON HOUSE–DAY–1936
He focuses on a distant rhythm, turning to the front door as a MULE WAGON rattles by.

INT. ROBINSON HOUSE–DAY–1936
He hears a CRICKET chirp. . .

INT. ROBINSON HOUSE–DAY–1936
Ray walks to the fireplace. . . then leans down and picks the cricket up. Aretha watches, amazed.

　　YOUNG RAY
　　I hear you, too, Mama.

Ray turns, walks up to Aretha, reaches out. . . and touches her cheek. Tears fill Aretha's eyes. . . .

　　YOUNG RAY *(cont'd)*
　　See. . . ? You're right there.

　　ARETHA
　　Yes, I am.

　　YOUNG RAY
　　Why're you cryin'?

　　ARETHA
　　Because I'm happy.

Aretha just holds her son. . .

CUT BACK TO:

EXT. HARLEM, NEW YORK–1952–DAY
Well-dressed urban Negroes chat after church, their kids running circles around them.

INT. SMALL HARLEM HOTEL–RAY'S ROOM–1952–DAY
A small phonograph plays a Gospel record as Ray sits all alone, reading his Braille Bible.

RAY
Now, after the death of Moses, it came to pass that the Lord spake unto Joshua. Be strong and of good courage, be not afraid. . .

A KNOCK at the door.

AHMET (V.O.)
Mr. Charles!

RAY
Who is it?!

AHMET (V.O.)
Mr. Charles, my name is Ahmet Ertegun. May I have a moment of your time?

RAY (yanks door open)
Man, I'm at church!

AHMET ERTEGUN—white, olive-skinned, late 20s—stands in the doorway.

AHMET
I'm sorry, I'll come back later —

RAY
You're here now. What do you want?

AHMET (beat)
Well. . . my company, Atlantic Records. . . has acquired your contract from Swingtime. (letting that sink in) I'd like to discuss your future. . .

RAY
Ain't no discussion, man. . . I ain't for sale!

AHMET
May I sit down?

Ray gestures okay. Ahmet enters cautiously. . .

AHMET (cont'd)
You see, Mr. Charles. . . Jack Lauderdale found himself, shall we say, a little over extended and had to unload

some of his talent. When your name came up, I jumped at the chance to work with you. I'm a big fan.

RAY (beat)
Yeah. . . ? Well, maybe I wanna go to another company.

AHMET (gently)
There is the small matter of a signed contract Jack sold us for $2500.

RAY
An' there is "the small matter" of you tellin' me 'bout my business!

AHMET
Yes. . . I'm sorry. I know that with some legal wrangling, you might find a way to break this contract. But why would you want to?

RAY (laughs)
It's simple, more money? I know a cat who'll pay me seven cents a record. Can you do that?

AHMET
Man, I could *say* I'd pay you fifteen cents a record, but I won't. . . any more than he'll pay you seven. But what I *will* do, is promise you five cents a record, and *pay* you five cents a record.

Ahmet stares at Ray, who just stands there silently.

AHMET (cont'd) (an appeal)
Mr. Charles, if you think pennies, you'll make pennies. But if you think dollars. . . you'll make dollars.

RAY
(I think millions, man). You know, I like the way you put things together. I dig you, Omelette.

AHMET
Ahmet.

RAY
What?

AHMET
Ahmet.

Ray shakes his hand. Ahmet smiles, relieved.

RAY
Ahmet. What kinda name is that?

AHMET
I'm Turkish.

RAY
Well, Ahmet, it looks like Jack's bad luck is my good fortune. . . 'cause I know Atlantic's a bigger label than Swingtime. Hell, I dig Atlantic. . . You guys make good records.

AHMET
You could've fooled me.

RAY *(shrugs)*
Sometimes, I gotta keep an eye on you city boys. *(smiling)* Down home, we call it "country dumb." *(offers him chicken)* Fried chicken. It ain't Turkish.

They both laugh.

EXT. NEW YORK CITY–TIMES SQUARE–NIGHT–1952

INT. ATLANTIC RECORDS RECORDING STUDIO–NIGHT–1952
During the day, Atlantic's office is the ramshackle war room of an upstart record company: At night, the desks are pushed against the walls to create a recording studio. As Ray and some studio musicians are recording "Roll with My Baby." Ahmet sits in a glassed-off closet/control room listening with TOM DOWD, a young, white recording engineer. . . and JESSE STONE, black, Atlantic's dapper arranger.

AHMET
What do you think?

JESSE *(shaking his head)*
Nobody wants another Nat King Cole.

MATCH DISSOLVE TO:

INT. ATLANTIC STUDIO CONTROL BOOTH–ANOTHER NIGHT–1952
Ahmet, Tom, and Jesse listen to Ray record "Midnight Hour."

JESSE *(dejected)*
Sounds just like Charles Brown.

AHMET *(standing up)*
I'll talk to him. . .

Tom stops the band.

TOM DOWD
That's a cut, fellas. . . Take five.

JESSE
He just don't get it. You either sound original or you got nothing.

Ahmet enters the studio, sits next to Ray.

RAY
Did you like that?

AHMET *(beat)*
Ray, I've got something to say. . . that I hope you won't take wrong.

RAY
Give it to me right, then.

Ahmet takes a deep breath, steeling himself.

AHMET
I signed you because I sensed something special in you. . . not because you sound like Nat Cole or Charles Brown.

RAY *(concerned)*
I thought you liked what I do. . .

AHMET
What we like. . . is the timbre of your voice. Your virtuosity, your energy.

A DONE DEAL

In 1952, we signed a man who was going to become one of the most important people in the history and development of Atlantic Records. One evening I was over at Herb and Miriam Abramson's house when they said, "We've got to play this for you," and they put on a record of Ray Charles. I said, "My God—he's fabulous!"

Ray was on a California label by the name of Swingtime, which was owned by Jack Lauderdale. At that time, I had a friend named Billy Shaw, who was an agent who booked a lot of R&B talent and did very well, but Billy didn't think he could book him. Finally, he said to me, "Look, why don't you record him? I would be able to book him if you made some good records." I said, "I guarantee we'll make some great records with him—how do I get him?" He said, "You buy his contract. Lauderdale is ready to sell. He wants $2,500." I said, "Done deal."

So we brought Ray to New York where he also got a job playing piano with the Joe Morris Band. . . . We took Ray into the studio and, as usual, I was producing the record. I wrote a couple of songs, Ray brought in a couple of songs written by other people, and we recorded all of this stuff with a pickup band. I wrote a song called "Heartbreaker" for one of Ray's first sessions with us. Around the same time, I also wrote "Mess Around" for him. Because of a studio tape that was floating around, a lot of fuss has been made about my singing this song to Ray so that he could memorize it and get the off-beat. We were just running through it, that's all. What was incredible about that session was that although Ray, I'm sure, knew about boogie-woogie piano playing, he had not at that time heard Cow Cow Davenport, one of the pioneers of that style. So in explaining "Mess Around," I was trying to put across to Ray the very precise phrasing of Cow Cow Davenport, when he suddenly began to play the most incredible example of that style of piano playing I've ever heard. It was like witnessing Jung's theory of the collective unconscious in action—as if this great artist had somehow plugged in and become

a channel for a whole culture that just came pouring out of him. I was trying to produce Ray the way we were recording Joe Turner or the Clovers. The records didn't do that well, but well enough so that he could go out on the road. That was when he started writing, so we didn't have to find material for him anymore. He would rehearse all his songs and when he said, "I am ready to record," we'd go into the studio, and he'd have "Hallelujah! I Love Her So," and all these terrific songs that he'd written. By the time we did "What'd I Say," which became like an anthem all over the country, Ray had become our first big, big star.

—Ahmet Ertegun,
What'd I Say

ABOVE: Ahmet Ertegun, circa 1950, from his book *What'd I Say*.
RIGHT: Curtis Armstrong is an amazing look-alike in the movie.

RAY
But not my music.

AHMET
I didn't say that, I —

RAY
This is what I do, Ahmet. *(subdued)* I gotta make a livin'. . . so I give the people what they want. I don't know no other way.

AHMET
Then we have to help you find one. *(beat)* Let's try a change of pace. . . are you familiar with stride piano?

RAY
You kiddin'? I learned how to play from a stride player.

AHMET
Well, I have this song. . . it's called "Mess Around."

RAY
Good title. . . who wrote it?

AHMET *(beat)*
I did.

RAY *(smiling)*
You did. Okay. . . sing it for me.

AHMET
Me. . . ?

RAY
It ain't like I can read the lyrics.

AHMET
Well. . . it's in the key of G. And it should have kind of a. . . Pete Johnson style.

Ray starts to play a propulsive, stride piano figure. . . and Ahmet begins to sing in a nasal monotone, with an accent that's hilarious.

AHMET *(cont'd)*
Well you can talk about the pit barbecue,
The band was jumpin', the people too,
They're doin' the Mess Around,
They're doin' the Mess Around,
They're doing the Mess Around.
Everybody's doin' the Mess Around. . . .

RAY
Now let me take it. . .

Starts to play. . .

MATCHED MUSIC AND PICTURE CUT TO:

INT. THE RED WING–DAY–1937
Mr. Pit accompanying Young Ray (already blind), playing a wild boogie-woogie duet at the Red Wing Cafe. . .

CUT BACK TO:

INT. ATLANTIC STUDIO–NIGHT–1952
. . . as Ray finishes playing "Mess Around". . .

JESSE
Now we got something.

AHMET
Pretty damn cool.

RAY
How was that, Ahmet?

AHMET
Great, Ray, great.

A WHITE GUY with dark hair, 30s, shouts from the doorway.

JERRY WEXLER
Unbelievable!!

Everyone busts up at JERRY WEXLER's signature line.

RAY *(turning to Ahmet)*
Who's that?

AHMET *(motioning Jerry over)*
Ray, I'd like you to meet my new partner, Jerry Wexler. He coined the term "rhythm and blues" at *Billboard Magazine*. . .

JERRY *(shaking Ray's hand)*
Ray Charles. I'm gonna sit back and watch and learn how to produce a record. . . I'm in awe man, totally outta sight, it's runnin' and riffin'.

AHMET
Yeah, Jerry always wanted to be the quiet, mysterious type. . . only he could never keep his mouth shut long enough.

Ray laughs. . . as he reprises the explosive intro to "Mess Around."

KING BEE (V.O.)
Alright, we're back at KCOH Houston with Atlantic artist Ray Charles.

INT. KCOH RADIO STUDIO (TEXAS)–DAY–1953
Ray sits with a black D.J., KING BEE, as "MESS AROUND" continues to play.

KING BEE
We're listening to the new Atlantic single "Mess Around" by Ray Charles and we have the gentleman here in the studio. So, Ray, when you're not makin' your own music. . . who do you listen to?

RAY
Fact is, King Bee, I really love gospel. An' one of my favorite groups is from right here in Houston. The Cecil Shaw Singers. . .

KING BEE
You heard it—Ray Charles endorses Houston's own Cecil Shaw. We'll be playin' gospel all day Sunday. . . but right now here's some more "Mess Around."

The phone RINGS. King Bee answers it.

KING BEE *(cont'd)* *(into phone)*
King Bee. . . sure, baby, right here. *(handing the phone to Ray)* Miss Della Antwine of The Cecil Shaw Singers.

RAY *(smooth as silk)*
Hello, Miss Antwine. . .

INT. THE CRYSTAL WHITE HOTEL RESTAURANT (TEXAS)– DAY–1953
DELLA ANTWINE, early 20s, dines with impeccable manners. Tall and shapely, she's a shy girl, very reserved. . . and Ray is trying to draw her out.

RAY
You sang tenor on "Jesus Is My Shepherd". . . right?

DELLA *(surprised)*
Yes, how'd you pick me out?

RAY
I lifted up my shades and looked at you. Actually, I hear like you see. Like that hummin' bird outside the window for instance. . .

Della glances up.

INT. RESTAURANT WINDOW–DAY–1953
A hummingbird flits around a window box.

INT. RESTAURANT–DAY–1953
Della sits back in her chair, impressed. Watches the hummingbird for a moment.

DELLA
I can't hear her. . .

RAY *(smiles)*
You gotta listen.

She tries again, focusing intently.

RAY *(cont'd)* *(beat)*
Hear that?

DELLA
What?

RAY
Her heart just skipped a beat.

Della looks at him a moment, then busts up laughing. Ray leans forward now, zeroing in for the kill.

RAY *(cont'd)*
You just gotta. . . be there, that's all. In this moment, right now.

They listen. Silence. Then, in the distance. . . the faint FLUT-TER of a hummingbird's wings.

RAY *(cont'd)*
Now Miss Antwine, can you hear it?

DELLA *(smiles)*
Yes. . .

RAY
See? Before, you were just listenin' to other things.

DELLA *(beat)*
To you. . .

An unspoken connection. Ray edges closer to her. . . his voice warm, intimate.

RAY *(softly)*
So. . . how'd you like my record? The one King Bee was playin'?

DELLA *(beat)*
It was. . . very nice.

That stops Ray cold. She's being polite, and he knows it.

DELLA *(cont'd) (covering)*
I. . . I've heard a lot of your music.

RAY
Was it very nice, too. . . ? *(off her silence)* If you don't like the record, you don't have to beat around the bush. My Mama always told me the truth.

Della hesitates. . . then sits back, putting her fork down.

DELLA
It's not that I don't enjoy your music. It's just that I feel. . . I've heard it before. I keep wonderin'. . . what

the real Ray Charles sounds like.

RAY
Ray Charles. . . *(a weary smile)* Who's he?

DELLA *(beat)*
Nobody. . . if you don't know.

That hits Ray.

RAY
I ain't made a dime soundin' like Ray Charles. . .

DELLA
Maybe that's true. . . but how successful can you be, soundin' like Nat Cole? Seems to me, folks'll always buy his records first.

An awkward silence as she waits for Ray's response.

DELLA *(cont'd) (troubled)*
Sorry. . . I should've kept my mouth shut.

RAY
No. . . it ain't like I never been told that before. Maybe I just. . . never listened.

He reaches out across the table. Tentatively she puts her hand in his. A delicate silence plays between them. . . until Della grows uneasy, she moves her hand away.

DELLA
Mr. Charles. . . I gotta go.

RAY *(standing up)*
I'll see you home.

DELLA
I live with a preacher's family.

RAY *(turns and walks away)*
I'll still see you home. . .

That makes Della smile. She's about to reach for his arm. . . when he takes off. She hurries after him.

LANDMARK MOMENTS

Ray Charles may not have been the first R&B singer to infuse gospel music into his sound, but he was certainly the first to make this style popular. Today, people don't understand how controversial this new hybrid sound was for the black community in the early 1950s. African Americans had never mixed God's music (gospel) with the devil's music (the blues) so when Ray Charles recorded "I Got a Woman," which was unabashedly gospel-influenced, people threatened to string him up. African-American preachers attacked him from the pulpit for having blasphemed. Of course, the music was only controversial because people were actually buying those records. When Ray followed up "I Got a Woman" with "Hallelujah, I Love Her So" and "A Fool for You," the African-American community enthusiastically made them hits.

How had Ray Charles stumbled on this revolutionary sound?

After beginning his career by copying other musicians and styles (Nat King Cole and Charles Brown for example), Ray realized that to make a name for himself, he'd have to come up with his own style. He'd grown up in the South loving both gospel and the blues. He knew that gospel records sold extremely well in the black community. So one day when he was driving from Louisiana to Texas with a trumpet player named Raynard Richards, Ray suggested that they break with tradition and write a song that combined the virtues of both gospel and blues. Charles and Richards wrote "I Got a Woman" and forever changed American musical culture.

In the film, we dramatized this historic moment in a scene with his future wife, Della Bea Antwine, who had told Ray when she first met him that he'd never make a name for himself sounding like Nat King Cole. Della was a gospel singer and was outraged at first when Ray played her his new composition. However, she fell in love with Ray and ultimately encouraged him to brave the attacks from the pulpit and pursue his new sound.

—Taylor Hackford

INT. RESTAURANT LOBBY–DAY–1953

DELLA *(concerned)*
Ray, the door's on the left—

RAY *(suddenly helpless)*
They moved the door?

Della takes his arm. Ray folds his arm around hers—immediate intimacy.

EXT. SEMI-URBAN NEIGHBORHOOD–HOUSTON–MOMENTS
LATER–DAY–1953
Ray and Della stroll down the sidewalk, arm in arm.

RAY
You know, you really a country girl.

DELLA
Yeah. . . how'd you know?

RAY
The way you ordered, "Let me get some molasses
with my cornbread."

Everything I do is natural, man. It's like somebody asking me, "Did you know this was going to be a hit?" I never thought about music that way. I've always wanted to do one thing: to make the music, in itself, as good as I can. Now, if it was fortunate enough to turn out to be a hit, fine. But then, I've done a lot of music that was not a hit but it was damn good music and I can listen to it today. A lot of times when I get on an airplane, people will come up to me and ask about some obscure song that I forgot I even did!

—Ray Charles, interview with Ashley Kahn, June 24, 2003

DELLA *(smiles)*
Were you raised on a farm?

RAY
My mama did some sharecroppin' in Florida.

DELLA
Is she still there?

RAY *(beat)*
God bless her soul. She passed away when I was at school.

DELLA
Ray. . . I'm sorry.

Silence. He draws her closer. . . remembering.

FLASHBACK TO:

EXT. JELLYROLL COUNTRY ROAD–DAY–1937
A soft wind blows across the green fields. We SEE Young Ray and
Aretha waiting for the bus. She puts an ID tag round his neck.

ARETHA
Somebody'll fetch you when the bus gets to St. Augustine.
When you get there, you show 'em this. Tell 'em your
name is Ray Charles Robinson.

Young Ray just looks up at his mother. It's all Aretha can do
to keep from crying.

ARETHA *(cont'd)*
An' the sandwiches I made, don't eat 'em all at once. . .
ya hear me?

Young Ray begins to tear up.

YOUNG RAY
Mama. . . please don't make me go away. I'll keep up
with the normal kids *(crying now)* I'll be good, jes' like
George. . .

Aretha fights back her emotions as she kneels down to face
him.

ARETHA
This got nothin' to do with George. . . *(wiping Ray's eyes)*
I've taken you as far as I can, baby. Them teachers in St.
Augustine know things I can't teach you. An' you need
an education in this world. . .

YOUNG RAY
I don't want no education!

ARETHA
Shhh, don't say that—

YOUNG RAY
I don't, I wanna stay here with you!

ARETHA *(takes him by the shoulders)*
Stop it, Ray! I won't have you livin' hand to mouth like
me—you hear?

The boy listens, nodding his head.

ARETHA *(cont'd)*
Now. . . if you wanna do somethin' to make your Mama
proud, promise me you'll never let nobody turn you into
no cripple. . . you won't become a charity case. . . an'
you'll always stand on your own two feet. . .

YOUNG RAY
I promise.

ARETHA *(squeezing Ray to her)*
I love you, baby. . . I'm so proud of you. . .

CUT BACK TO:

EXT. HOUSTON RESIDENTIAL NEIGHBORHOOD–DAY–1953
Ray and Della walk along in silence for a moment.

DELLA
Your mother sounds like an amazing woman.

RAY
She didn't want me to be carryin' no tin cup. . .
that's for sure. *(beat)* Most of the kids I went to
school with do basket weavin' an' wicker work.

DELLA
But not you. Because of your gift.

RAY
'Cause of my ears. *(a weary laugh)* I can mimic
damn near anybody. Make a pretty decent livin' at
it, too. But if I change my style, an' people don't dig
it. . . what am I left with? *(beat)* When you're blind,
Miss Antwine. . . you ain't got that many choices.

DELLA
Seems to me, you got all the choices in the world. God
gave you the gift to sound like anybody you please. . .
(pointedly) . . . even yourself.

That hits Ray. Della slows her pace.

DELLA *(cont'd)*
We're here. . . this is where I live.

RAY *(that slow smile)*
Think the preacher might let me in. . . ? I need
a little prayer.

DELLA *(tentatively)*
His wife don't like me havin' male company. . .

RAY
Tell 'em it's Nat King Cole. *(beat)* Ya know, Miss Antwine
. . . you really got me thinkin'.

DELLA
'Bout what. . . ?

RAY
About my music. . . about my life. About many things. . .

Ray gently takes her face in his hands. . . and kisses her on
the lips. After a moment, their embrace deepens. Finally,
Della steps back. . . .

DELLA
Ray. . . aren't you movin' a little too fast?

RAY
I thought I was moving pretty smooth. *(beat)* I'm goin'
up to New York for a couple weeks. When I come back
. . . we'll take it as slow as you want.

DELLA *(blushes, charmed)*
alright, Mr. Charles.

They just stand there a moment. . . neither of them wanting
to part. He wants to say more. . . but he can't find the words.

RAY *(softly)*
Alright, Miss Antwine. . . See ya in a couple weeks. . .

He starts to walk off.

DELLA
Wait. I'll call you a cab.

Ray saunters off.

RAY
Three blocks up, left for two blocks, right for one more. . .
an' then fifteen giant steps and I'm at the Crystal White
Hotel.

EXT. NEW YORK CITY–MIDTOWN–1953 (STOCK)–DAY

INT. ATLANTIC RECORDS OFFICE–DAY–1953
The studio is an office again, the mikes and recording equipment pushed against the walls. Ahmet and Jerry sit at desks that face each other. . . but they're listening to Ray.

AHMET
"Mess Around" was a positive step for us, Ray. We're making progress.

RAY
Atlantic's been real good to me, but I ain't givin' you cats no hits. If I'm gonna create somethin' special, I'm gonna need my own band.

AHMET (alarmed)
Ray. . . taking a band on the road costs a bundle. Even Joe Morris is struggling, and his band's had a hit record.

RAY
You want me to create somethin' special, right? Well, I need my own band to do that. (I'm not Joe Morris, man.) You said think pennies, you'll make pennies. I'm thinkin' dollars, man. . .

Ahmet smiles at the irony of his own words, coming back at him.

JERRY (to Ahmet)
Ruth Brown's got a tour booked in Georgia—she needs a band.

RAY
I'll take it. I can do her charts, back her up, an' be the openin' act.

AHMET
Okay. . . but you're gonna be responsible. You gotta make it pay.

I really think they (Atlantic Records) were phenomenal about hearing talent—most of us who came to Atlantic, what we were doing was raw, it was raw stuff, it really was. I think they had this feeling for the music and they never got in the way of my music, never, at no point from start to finish. They would submit songs to me but they never once said, "Record this." There was never a time there was any pressure.

—Ray Charles

An advertisement from Atlantic Records in *Cash Box*, dated June 28, 1956, includes Ray Charles in what was probably one of his first appearances in print.

95

RAY
I'm gonna make it do what it do, baby. . .

Ray's elated, but Ahmet and Jerry aren't convinced.

CUT TO:

EXT. THE PREACHER'S HOUSE (HOUSTON)–DAY–1953
Della looks through the window and sees Ray outside. She opens the door.

RAY
Miss Antwine. . . it's been two weeks.

DELLA
It's been three.

Della smiles. . . surprising Ray with a kiss.

RAY
What about the preacher an' his wife. . . ?

DELLA
They're in Dallas till Monday.

Della pulls Ray into the house.

INT. PREACHER'S HOUSE–DELLA'S BEDROOM–DAY–1953
Ray and Della lie in bed, still glowing from their lovemaking.

RAY
Della Bea, huh? That's like a honey bee, right?

She laughs.

RAY *(cont'd)*
Can I call you Bea. . . ?

DELLA
Yeah. . . I'd like that.

RAY *(beat)*
Ya know. . . there's only two cats that I've ever really

trusted in my life. Jeff Brown, he's gonna be my road manager, and Fathead Newman, my tenor man. And now, you. *(he reveals his scarred eyes)* Do me a favor, Bea. You always gotta always tell me the truth. Like you did before. Don't feel sorry for me just 'cause I'm blind.

DELLA
How could I pity someone I admire. . . ?

That makes Ray smile. He sits up in bed.

RAY
Can I play somethin' for you?

DELLA
Now?. . .

How do you reconstruct genius? He took the Lord's music and the devil's words and made this amalgam they call soul music. And as a performer, there is no one you can compare him to, and the distance to whoever is second is immeasurable. That's the way it is with Bob Dylan and Aretha Franklin in their areas. No one has ever performed at the piano with as much charisma as Ray Charles.

—Jerry Wexler, *The Los Angeles Times*, June 11, 2004

INT. PREACHER'S HOUSE–PARLOR PIANO–MOMENTS
LATER–1953
Della helps Ray to the piano. He sits down.

DELLA
Go ahead, play. I'm gonna close these drapes.

As she closes the drapes her face shows concern and she tries to get his attention.

DELLA *(cont'd)* *(during song)*
Ray. . . Ray. . .

RAY *(singing)*
**I got a woman, way over town,
good to me, oh yeah. . . I got a woman. . .
way over town. . . she's good to me. . .
oh yeah, she gives me money when
I'm in need. . .**

Her words finally stop him.

DELLA
Ray. . . that's sacrilegious.

RAY
What. . . ?

DELLA
It's a gospel song.

RAY
I know what it is. I wrote it. You told me to find my own voice. Bea, this is it. . . .

DELLA
But it ain't right, changin' gospel into. . . this.

RAY
This what. . . ? Devil music? Evil music? I ain't evil, Bea. I grew up singin' gospel an' blues. It's who I am. . . an' if I'm gonna do my own thing, it's gotta be natural, right? I'm singin' 'bout my feelin'. . . for you. What could be more natural than that?

DELLA *(touched)*
Ray. . .

She touches his scarred eyes and hugs him.

Della has to smile. Despite herself, she's charmed.

CUT TO:

EXT. ROYAL PEACOCK NIGHTCLUB–ATLANTA–DAY

INT. ROYAL PEACOCK NIGHTCLUB–ATLANTA–DAY–1954
CLOSE UP: Ruth Brown singing "5 10 15"

A curvy woman shattering crystal with her bluesy wail. Ray pounds out chord progressions on the piano, the band thundering around him. Fathead Newman blows a sax solo.

Suddenly, Ruth falls. Jeff rushes over to help her.

RUTH BROWN
Jeff, get me away from the boys.

As he helps her to a chair.

RAY (nodding toward Ruth)
Jeff. What's up, man?

JEFF
One second, Boss, Ruth's not feeling so good.

Jeff Brown, in a new suit, leads Ray over to Ruth.

RAY (patting her shoulder)
You alright, Ruth?

RUTH (beat)
Ray, I ain't slept a wink. . . my innards are churnin' and I'm pukin' up everythin' I eat.

RAY
You gotta take a rest, baby. . .

RUTH
Ray, I'm pregnant with Clyde McPhatter's baby. Ahmet and Jerry are gonna be pissed. . . me and "The Drifters" are Atlantic's two biggest sellers.

RAY
Nah, baby, they'll be cool. . . probably make the whole thing into a big publicity stunt.

Ruth takes a deep breath. . . steeling herself.

RUTH
You think so? I'm sorry, daddy-o, I can't finish out the tour.

Ruth gets up and walks out of the club. Ray's devastated.

JEFF
What're we gonna do, boss?

RAY
I can't let this go. . .

He turns back to the band.

RAY (cont'd)
Ruth ain't gonna make the tour. We only got four days to rehearse my sound till they throw our asses outta here, so we're gonna kick it 'round the clock. (off their silence) Anybody who thinks that's too much work, there's the door. Jeff'll pay your bus fare home.

Fathead walks over and grabs his sax.

FATHEAD
Let's hear what ya got, daddy.

The other musicians take up their positions. Ray smiles and starts to lay out a groove on the piano.

EXT. ROYAL PEACOCK NIGHTCLUB–ATLANTA–DAY–1954
Ahmet and Jerry jump out of a taxi and dash across the street.

"Ray called me and said, 'I'm doing this movie,'" Ruth Brown said, recalling one of her last conversations with Charles, an old band mate. "He said, 'Who do you want to play you?' and I said, 'Halle Berry, you crazy fool!' He said, 'I ain't that blind.'"

—The New York Times, July 20, 2004

INT. ROYAL PEACOCK NIGHTCLUB–ATLANTA–RAINY
DAY–1954
Ahmet and Jerry walk through the door.

> AHMET
> I'll leave you to break this to Ray. . .

> JERRY
> You're gonna let me break this to Ray? Why?

> AHMET
> Because Ruth Brown was your idea.

> JERRY
> Ruth Brown was a good idea.

ON STAGE

> JEFF
> Boss, they're here.

> RAY
> Let's show 'em what we've got.

Ray counts out a downbeat and the waiting band jumps into

GETTING THE LOOK: PRODUCTION DESIGN

As for the locations, I try to get away from making the movie look like other movies that have come before. Places like New York, Los Angeles, or Wilmington, North Carolina, have been filmed so many times that you are basically re-using the same locations over and over again. We shot most of *Ray* in New Orleans, which is rarely used in film and the exteriors were really fresh.
—Stephen Altman, production designer

"I Got a Woman." The two producers are stunned: This is the new Ray Charles. . . with his own unique style. Ray has finally found his voice. Ahmet has to sit. Jerry stands there, dazed.

> JERRY
> Ahmet. . .

> AHMET
> Yeah.

> JERRY
> We gotta get this on wax. . .

Soul is when you take a song
and make it part of you—a part
that's so true, so real, people
think it must have happened
to you. . . . It's like electricity:
we don't really know what it
is, do we? But it's a force that
can light a room. Soul is like
electricity, like a spirit,
a drive, a power.

—Ray Charles, *Life,* July 29, 1966

AHMET
Oh yeah. . .

CUT TO:

INT. WINS RADIO STUDIO–DAY–MUSIC CONTINUES–1954
An Atlantic 45RPM record spins on a turntable as the MUSIC CONTINUES.

ALAN FREED (V.O.)
Hear that New York? The sound is huge. . .

ALAN FREED turns up "I Got a Woman," and shouts into the mike:

ALAN FREED *(cont'd)*
. . . but there's only seven cats on this record! This is the new Ray Charles, baby. . . and there's nothin' out there like it! And you heard it first on the Moondog Show!

Jerry sits behind Freed in the booth. He takes out a white envelope and slips it into Freed's jacket pocket.

EXT. NEW YORK CITY–1954–DAY–STOCK

AHMET (V.O.)
We've got to get your band out on the road. . . and the Shaw Agency is the best booker on the Chitlin Circuit.

INT. ATLANTIC OFFICES–DAY–1954
Ahmet leads Ray in to MILT SHAW, 30s, a hip young man in a shiny suit who boldly shakes Ray's hand.

When I wrote this song, "I Got a Woman," I decided now is the time. Either you're going to sink or swim. So at that point I just said, "Hey, this is what I'm going to do and if I'm going to be accepted, good, and at least if I'm not going to be accepted, I'll know that, too.

—Ray Charles

AHMET
That's my opinion. . . Milt Shaw, I want you to meet Ray Charles. Milt's dad, Billy, was the one who first called my attention to a certain blind pianist when he was booking Lowell Fulson.

MILT SHAW
Ray Charles. . . We believe in your talent. . . we want to be in the Ray Charles business. I've already got you booked on a ten-city tour with Roy Milton's Solid Senders and Tangula, the Exotic Shake Dancer.

AHMET
She's gorgeous. I gotta tell you, Ray, I believe you're onto something very big. Nobody's ever combined R&B with gospel before. . . "I Got a Woman" is a smash. . . you've got to start thinking about a follow-up my friend—like, now.

RAY
That all sounds good, but I'm on my way to Texas to take care of some business, but I'll be right back.

MILT SHAW
Better make it fast. I'm ready to sell, sell, sell.

RAY
As long as you put me in front of Tangula. . . Jeff.

Ray and Jeff leave.

MILT SHAW
Incredible, are you sure he's blind? I think he's pulling a fast one on us.

AHMET
He's an amazing cat.

EXT./INT. RAY AND DELLA'S NEW HOME–HOUSTON–DAY–1954
A "JUST MARRIED" sign adorns the trunk on Ray's new Ford, tin cans tied to the bumper. Fathead, the band and their girl-friends run up the steps of a Houston bungalow, laughing, throwing rice at Ray and Della. Jeff runs back to the car to get his camera. Ray picks Della up.

DELLA *(dubious)*
Ray, are you sure about this?

RAY
I got you.

Ray misses the front door. . . and walks Della right into the wall. Their wedding guests laugh hysterically.

DELLA
Ray?!

RAY
I can do it, Bea.

ALL AD LIBS THRU SCENE.

Ray makes another attempt. . . and with Della's help, they stumble through the front door. . . SLAMMING it on wedding guests who're doubled over in laughter.

DISSOLVE TO:

EXT. RAY & DELLA'S HOUSTON HOME–DAY–1954
Time lapse dissolve establishing.

INT. RAY & DELLA'S SMALL BEDROOM (TEXAS) DAY–1954
Close-up: RAY opens a kerchief and takes out his "works"—heroin capsules, spoon, needle, and lighter.

DELLA (V.O.)
Ray. . . can I come in?

Ray freezes for an instant. . . then shoves his works into a drawer.

RAY
Hold on, baby. . . I'm comin'.

He unlocks the door and Della nearly flies at him, playfully tackling him onto the bed. She kisses him. . . then, her face grows serious:

DELLA *(softly)*
Why you lockin' doors on me, Ray. . . ?

RAY *(beat)*
It's a small house. . . shouldn't we both get a lil' privacy?

DELLA
Maybe we should both get a lil' more *room*. . . *(beat)*

We're gonna need some space, when we start a family.

Family? The word troubles Ray. . . but he tries not to let on.

RAY
Ya know. . . I'm gonna be on the road, most of the year.

Della studies him. . . concerned now.

DELLA
Ray?

COSTUMES

On the same day we might shoot scenes that took place in three different time periods. Consequently, we had an enormous amount of wardrobe—five trailers full of clothes.

When we were moving the clothes to Baton Rouge from New Orleans, I got a call to say that one of the trailers was on fire. Everything burned up. All that was left of the clothing was ashes. It was a huge loss. Fortunately, the clothes that burned were all sixties outfits for the extras, which was much easier to replace than the costumes from the thirties, forties, or fifties.

—Sharen Davis, costume designer

RAY *(subdued)*
What if I'm not a good father? My daddy was never around. He had three different families. . .

DELLA
Well, we're gonna have one. And soon. . . right now.

She kisses him playfully.

INT. EBONY LOUNGE–NIGHT–1955

RAY *(singing)*
**If I call her on the telephone,
tell her that I'm all alone,
By the time I count from one to four,
I hear her —**

Ray hesitates as the drummer bangs out 1,2,3,4 —

RAY *(cont'd)*
—on my door. In the evenin' when the sun goes down, when there's nobody else around, she kisses me an' she holds me tight, an' tells me "Daddy, everything's all right" . . . that's why I know, yes I know, Hallelujah, I Love Her So!

Suddenly, a husband and wife in the audience stand up and angrily shout Ray down.

ANGRY HUSBAND
Y'all crazy, sittin' up here, listenin' to this devil!

Jeff jumps in as others in the audience try to shut him up.

ANGRY WIFE
Y'all givin' your money to Satan!

RAY *(stopping the band)*
You got a problem. . . ?

ANGRY HUSBAND
Yeah, I got a problem—that's gospel you're singin'! You're turnin' God's music into sex, makin' money off the Lord!

ANGRY WIFE *(pointing to the band)*
Don't y'all smile at me. . . y'all part of it, too. All of y'all are gonna burn in hell!

BASS PLAYER (STANDING UP)
She's right. . .

FATHEAD
Robert, cool down, man. . .

BASS PLAYER
No, man. . . this whole thing is wrong.

Robert, the bass player, swaggers offstage. The man and his wife cheer, heading for the exit, exhorting others to follow them. Jeff jumps onto the stage, strides up to Ray.

JEFF *(quietly)*
Wanna cancel the show. . . ?

RAY
I'm not gonna cancel the show. You just find us a bass player for tomorrow night. *(turning to the audience)* If you folks want more. . . gimme a "A-men!"

A loud "AMEN!" echoes in response. Ray laughs, grabs Jeff.

THE EBONY LOUNGE

We always do a lot of research. We compile as much material as possible and distribute it to all the departments so we all know basically what we are trying to achieve. We ran a lot of tests to decide what would look good and what we really wanted, and what we didn't want. But we didn't have any hard and fast rules and, of course, we are not making a documentary. There were not a whole lot of photographs from the time and place of this movie. We couldn't find photos of places like The Ebony Lounge, for example, so we had to make that up. We did follow Ray's band pictures but very often we had to improvise. We stayed as true to the feeling and spirit of the time as possible.

—Stephen Altman, production designer

RAY *(cont'd)*
While you're at it, find me a singer. A woman. . . somebody church-trained, but with no church attitude . . . dig?

Jeff nods, and Ray rolls right back into "Hallelujah."

CUT TO:

EXT. BLACK BAPTIST CHURCH–DAY–1955

> **BAPTIST MINISTER** (V.O.)
> This is a colored man bringin' the wrath of God
> down on other colored people. . . shamin' us all. . .
> stealin' riches from the Lord an' usin' 'em for the
> Devil's work!

INT. BLACK BAPTIST CHURCH–DAY–1955–MUSIC CONTINUES
An imposing, black BAPTIST MINISTER hurls fire and brim-
stone down at his congregation. . . where a pregnant Della
sits stoically, holding back the tears.

> **BAPTIST MINISTER**
> It's as outrageous as Simon the Magician, offerin'
> money to Peter for the shroud of the Holy Ghost.
> An' like Simon, Ray Charles will burn in hell!

EXT. RAY AND DELLA'S HOUSTON HOME–DAY–1955
Della walks home, bearing the weight of her pregnancy. . .
and the minister's words. Then, she looks up. . . and sees Ray,
sitting on the porch. Della throws open the garden gate,
rushing toward him.

> **DELLA** (excited)
> Ray! What're you doin' home. . . ?!

> **RAY**
> Our gig's just down in San Antonio, an' Jeff
> said he'd drive me down here. . . so here I am.
> (smiles) I got nine hours with you. . . .

> **DELLA** (throwing her arms around him)
> Nine hours, nine minutes, I don't care. . . long as
> you're here.

> **RAY** (Ad lib)
> What we got here?

> **DELLA** (ad lib)
> A little something in the oven. C'mon inside,
> we got a lot to do.

CUT TO:

INT. RAY AND DELLA'S LIVING ROOM–DAY–1955
A DARK CONTOUR—Della's pregnant belly, smooth as black
satin in the pale light filtering through the curtains. Ray's
hand gently caresses her roundness.

> **DELLA**
> I love the way you touch me. . .

> **RAY** (caressing her face)
> It's the way I see you, Bea.

Della smiles. For a moment, they lie there together in silence.

> **RAY** (cont'd)
> Ya know. . . I'm having trouble on this tour.
> 'Bout mixin' this gospel music with the blues. . .

> **DELLA** (feigning ignorance)
> Really?

> **RAY** (beat)
> I know I ain't no saint. . . but they treated me
> like I'm the devil himself. An' I believe in the
> same God they believe in. . .

Della studies Ray a moment. His pain is almost palpable.

> **DELLA**
> Ray, come here.

He moves closer to her.

> **DELLA** (cont'd)
> Ray. . . have your records stopped sellin'?

> **RAY**
> No, Ahmet says record sales are great.

> **DELLA**
> Yeah. . . ever since you blended gospel with
> your music. Blessin's come from God, Ray. An'
> He don't bless what He's against. . .

> **RAY**
> You might be the best thing that ever happened to me.

DELLA
I believe I am.

EXT. RAY & DELLA'S HOUSTON HOME–DAY–1955
Jeff drives up and honks the horn.

INT. RAY AND DELLA'S HOME–LIVING ROOM/BATHROOM–
DAY–1955
Della comes down the stairs with a fresh change of clothes.
Ray is sitting on the sofa.

DELLA
Ray, you got your watch? Blue shirts are on top,
pants in between, white shirts on the bottom. Here
are your glasses.

She hands him his glasses and starts putting the shirts in the
suitcase. He steps up behind her, kisses her neck.

RAY
Come on the road with me. . . ?

DELLA (beat)
Baby. . . what would I do on the road?

RAY
Do what I tell you, that's what. I've been looking to add
a female voice to the band anyway.

DELLA (laughs)
Can't you jes' see me, wobblin' around on that stage,
big as a house?

RAY (puts his arms around her)
I'll tell you what I see. . .

He kisses her neck.

DELLA (laughing)
Don't start what you can't finish . . . Jeff's waitin'.

Della playfully pushes him away and he exaggerates her
strength, flopping onto the couch. Della starts up the steps
again.

DELLA (cont'd) (gently)
I can't go on the road. Not with your baby inside me.

She scurries into the bathroom.

DELLA (V.O.) *(cont'd)*
I'll get your shavin' kit.

Ray jumps to his feet.

RAY
Bea, no! No, that's okay. . . .Hold on a second. . .

WE FOLLOW Ray as he scrambles into the bathroom: Della just stands there, dumbfounded. . . holding his heroin needle in her hands.

RAY *(cont'd)*
Bea. . . let me get it. . .

DELLA *(her voice trembling)*
How long you been hidin' this from me. . . ?

He doesn't know what to say.

DELLA *(cont'd)*
Ray. . . I'm your wife!

RAY *(subdued)*
I was so excited to come and see you Bea. . .
I forgot to leave it with the band.
(off Della's silence) Let me have it.

He reaches out, takes the shaving kit from her hands.

RAY *(cont'd)*
Bea, it's like. . . medicine to me. That's all.

DELLA
This ain't *medicine* to nobody! Don't be lyin'
to yourself!

RAY
But it ain't like I'm dealin' the stuff. I just use it
to get a little taste now an' then, that's all. . .

DELLA
You don't *taste* poison, Ray. . . it kills people!
Ya gotta stop!

RAY *(exploding)*
I ain't gonna do a goddamned thing!

His outburst silences Della for a moment. She glares up at Ray defiantly. . . shocked, hurt. Tears fill her eyes.

DELLA
What about me. . . what about our baby?

RAY *(trying to calm himself)*
Bea. . . it ain't like I'm new to this. If I ever felt it would jeopardize my music. . . or providin' for you and the baby. . . I'd stop it in a minute. But I know it won't. . .

Della's tears turn to sobs.

DELLA
How do you know that, Ray?

RAY *(a tortured moment)*
Because I know. You can talk till you're blue in the face but I ain't gonna stop.

Della looks up at him desperately. Downstairs, Jeff knocks at the door.

DELLA
I'm comin' with you.

RAY *(beat)*
No. . . no. . .

DELLA *(stunned)*
What. . . ? You just said a second ago—

RAY *(interrupting)*
It be just like you said, Bea. I don't think the road is a place for you an' the baby.

DELLA *(beat)*
What're you sayin' to me, Ray. . . ?

RAY
That I hope you'll be here for me. . . when I come home.

Della just stands there. . . devastated.

RAY *(cont'd)* *(walking out the door)*
Jeff, get my suitcase.

Jeff enters and starts to pick up Ray's bag. He greets Della cautiously.

JEFF
Hey, Della Bea. See you soon, alright.

Della's look says it all as he takes the bag and leaves.

FADE TO BLACK:

INT. SANDPIPER LOUNGE–DAY–1955

MARY ANN *(singing)*
It brings a tear to my eyes,
when I begin to realize,
I cried so much since you been gone. . . .

Ray and Jeff sit in the empty club listening to MARY ANN FISHER—shapely, early 20s—as she belts out an up-tempo jump version of "Drown in My Own Tears."

MARY ANN *(cont'd)*
I think I'll drown in my own tears. . .

Ray applauds and Mary Ann falls silent.

RAY
Great. . . I dig that. What's your name again, sweetheart?

MARY ANN
Mary Ann. . . Mary Ann Fisher.

RAY
Mary Ann. . . how'd you feel if I asked you to sing a torch song. . . with a gospel feel to it?

MARY ANN *(smiles)*
Gospel's all 'bout love, anyway. . . ain't it?

RAY
Wouldn't make you feel like a sinner?

MARY ANN
Mr. Charles, I love God an' he loves me. . . but
I ain't been to church since the Rev knocked-up
my cousin's wife.

RAY *(laughs)*
Hello, it's hard to find preacher clothes for a miserable
man, ain't it?

Ray holds out his hand and Mary Ann shakes it. Almost
unconsciously, Ray TOUCHES HER WRIST. Jeff watches
uneasily.

RAY *(cont'd)*
Let's say we rehearse this song a little bit. . .

JEFF
Boss, we got to go. . .

RAY *(cutting him off)*
Go 'head, we're gonna rehearse.

JEFF
You sure. . .

Ray waves him away sits at the piano. . . and Mary Ann
leans forward. Jeff watches them, then slowly walks away.

DISSOLVE TO:

INT. SANDPIPER LOUNGE–DAY–LATER–1955
Ray's hands coaxing soulful gospel chords from the keys.

RAY
**It brings a tear to my eyes,
when I begin to realize,**

Ray and Mary Ann are alone now in the empty club.

RAY *(cont'd)*
I cried so much, since you been gone. . .

Ray has transformed Mary Ann's arrangement of "Drown in
My Own Tears" into a slow, steamy blues that has sex drip-
ping off every note.

RAY *(cont'd)*
I think I'll drown in my own tears. . .

Ray's voice falls silent, but the piano throbs sensually as
he plays on. Mary Ann stands over him, hands on the
piano. . . feeling the tremor of his music. The girl is completely turned on.

MARY ANN
You're amazin'. . .

RAY
So are you, baby. . . come sit next to me.

She sits down now, rubbing her thigh provocatively against
his. Ray gets a whiff of her hair. . . her scent.

RAY (CONT'D)
So, what do you think?

Mary Ann turns Ray's face to hers. . . and kisses him as he
continues to play.

FADE TO BLACK:

INT. RAY'S HOTEL ROOM–NEW ORLEANS–NIGHT–1955–MUSIC CONTINUES
A MATCH FLARES. . . cooking heroin in a spoon as the MUSIC CONTINUES. We hear a KNOCK at a door.

> **JEFF** (V.O.)
> Ray, telephone.

> **RAY**
> Take a message.

> **JEFF** (V.O.)
> It's Della Bea.

Ray, silhouetted by streetlight, blows out the match and rises from his bed, concerned.

> **RAY**
> Tell her I'm busy.

> **JEFF** (V.O.)
> C'mon, man, I ain't lyin' to Bea!

Mary Ann sits up behind Ray.

> **MARY ANN**
> Uh-oh. . . is that the wife?

> **RAY**
> Shut up. . . *(to Jeff)* . . . I'll be there in a second.

Mary Ann smiles and lies back down. Ray starts to get dressed.

> **RAY** *(cont'd)*
> Don't mess with this junk, alright? All it'll do is make ya sick. . .

CUT TO:

INT. DELLA'S HOSPITAL ROOM–DAY–1955
A tiny, newborn hand grabs a hold of Ray's finger.

> **RAY**
> He's got all his fingers. . . an' toes?

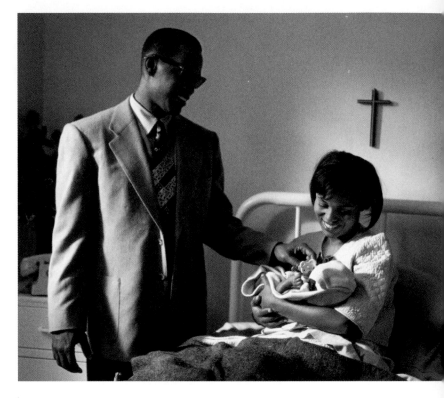

Della lies in bed, cradling her infant son, RAY CHARLES ROBINSON, JR. Ray hovers over them nervously. . .

> **DELLA**
> Yes.

> **RAY** *(apprehensively)*
> Can he. . . see?

> **DELLA**
> Yes. . .

Ray begins to relax, now.

> **DELLA** *(cont'd)*
> You want to hold him?

He does. . . but he's afraid.

> **DELLA** *(cont'd)*
> C'mon now. That's what you came here for. *(handing him the baby)* This is your daddy. . .

RAY *(in awe)*
My God. . . he ain't no bigger than a loaf of bread.

Della laughs. Ray just sits there a moment as the reality of fatherhood begins to sink in. He doesn't know what to say. Finally, he turns to Della.

RAY *(cont'd)*
Thank you. . . .

She smiles wearily.

DELLA
He's not my gift to you, Ray. He's your son.

RAY *(to the baby)*
I'm gonna take care of both of y'all. . . you know that, right?

Della looks up at him. . . sadness in her eyes.

RAY *(cont'd) (beat)*
I love you, Bea.

DELLA *(subdued)*
An' I love you, too. . . *(beat)* But there's somethin' I gotta say. I know you're a workin' musician, but don't bring the road into our home ever again, Ray. . . the home I'm makin' for you an' our children.

RAY
I won't. . . I promise.
(gently) But there's some things. . .

He stops himself.

DELLA
Don't say no more, okay? I ain't no fool. . .

Ray just sits there with his baby in his arms, wanting to tell her he'll be good. . . knowing he can't. So instead. . .

RAY
You're the only woman I'll ever love, Bea.

Della looks up at Ray. . . desperate to believe that. Jeff enters and starts taking pictures.

INT. CROOKED ACE–NIGHT–1955–MUSIC BEGINS
SEE LYRIC SHEET

RAY
Mary Ann, girl you sho' look fine. . .

Ray's dusky voice coos suggestive lyrics. . . as Mary Ann moves sensually to his music.

INT. RAY & DELLA'S KITCHEN–DAY–1955
They are bathing a baby Ray Jr.

EXT. HOUSTON NEIGHBORHOOD–DAY–1956–
MUSIC CONTINUES
Ray and Della push a baby buggy through their neighborhood.

EXT. SMALL TOWN, THE DEEP SOUTH–DAY–1956–MUSIC CONTINUES

Ray's Ford sedan rolls through a Southern town with the Band's DeSoto wagon in tow.

INT. RAY'S '54 FORD–DAY–1956–MUSIC CONTINUES

Jeff drives. He glances at the rearview mirror: In the back seat, Mary Ann is all over Ray. . . kissing his face, his neck.

> JEFF
> I'm trying to avoid the traffic speed traps. I think we're gonna be a little late.

> RAY
> Whatever. Stay within the limits.

> MARY ANN *(softly)*
> Why don't we get us a spot in Memphis? We'd have our own place. . .

> RAY
> I ain't leavin' Houston.

> MARY ANN *(starts to go down)*
> I bet she don't do this. . .

> RAY *(stops her)*
> Listen, every good-bye doesn't mean gone. I'm not leavin' my family.

Mary Ann's ambition isn't slowed at all.

> MARY ANN
> Okay, baby, no need to get sore. *(stroking his body)* Sugar. . . how 'bout given me a little more to do in the show? How 'bout a solo?

> RAY
> Girl, you don't quit', do ya? *(Mary Ann giggles)* I gotta fly up to New York to do some publicity, why don't you take a week off and look for some material. . . we'll talk when I get back.

HOLD ON RAY'S FACE. . . as Mary Ann kisses him, gliding downward, below the frame. He knows he's got big trouble.

114

The great artist uses no effects. Every innuendo is in fine rhythm and is part of Charles' personal story. . . When his music is happy, it's glorious in the happiness of self-expressions. When he is sad, his pleas are the cries of a man in pain, and when they are angry, it is the anger of the multitude. . . . It is his insight, his imagination, and artistry as compared to the musical sterility of a simple entertainer which makes him different and makes him click with the public, all people, all races, all classes, all backgrounds.
—Elgin Hychew, *Louisiana Weekly*, December 6, 1958

EXT. BUSY NYC STREET–DAY–1956
Ahmet and Jerry walk down 8th Ave. with Ray.

JERRY
They loved it. . . They loved you, Ray. . . We're gonna get the cover of *Billboard.*

RAY *(preoccupied)*
Listen, man, I wanna do a session while I'm here. How 'bout tomorrow?

AHMET
You got the band up here?

RAY
The band here. . . everyone 'cept Mary Ann.
I'm gonna need some new background, though.
I been hearin' this thing in my head. . . kinda a dance between a man an' three women.

AHMET
Sounds nice, can I watch?

RAY
A dance of voices, Ahmet.

AHMET
What kind of voices? Like Mary Ann?

RAY *(killing that idea)*
Her voice is too. . . smooth for what I'm hearin'. I need a sound that's. . . raw.

JERRY *(eyes connecting with Ahmet's)*
The Cookies. . .

RAY
Cookies are sweet. . .

CUT TO:

The original Cookies, from top: Margie Hendricks, Ethel "Earl-Jean" McRae, and Pat Lyles.

INT. ATLANTIC RECORDS RECORDING STUDIO–NIGHT–1956

RAY (V.O.) *(singing)*
If you don't want, you don't have to. . .

THE COOKIES: ETHEL McRAE, PAT LYLES, and MARGIE HEN-DRICKS—black and sexy—are backing up Ray's "Leave My Woman Alone."

THE COOKIES
. . . get in trouble. . .

RAY & THE COOKIES
If you don't want,
you don't have to get in trouble. . .
If you don't want,
you don't have to get in trouble. . .
You'd better leave my woman alone.

RAY
Well, I know you're a playboy,
Breakin' hearts all over town,
But if you touch my little girl,
I'm gonna lay your body down. . . .

INT. CONTROL ROOM–NIGHT–1956
Ahmet, Jerry, and Tom sit, soaking up this sensual new sound.

TOM
He's on fire. . .

JERRY
Maybe we should sign these girls up.

AHMET
If I know Ray, we won't get the chance.

RAY & THE COOKIES (V.O.)
You better leave. . . my woman alone. . .

Ray is scatting, performing a vibrant call and response with the group. He turns his ear to Margie. . .and the other girls' voices begin to FADE AWAY. In a moment, MARGIE'S SINGING is the ONLY SOUND Ray hears. She's got it—the raw power.

The song ends. All applaud. Merriam pushes past Jerry.

JERRY
Goddammit, Merriam, our office at night, your office during the day.

DISSOLVE TO:

INT. ATLANTIC RECORDS RECORDING
STUDIO–NIGHT/LATER–1956
The Raelettes crowd around the piano as the take is being played back. Ethel and Pat are thrilled by the sound, but Margie remains aloof.

RAY
I love it, we're gonna put it out.

ETHEL
Ya know. . . I never got a record in one take before.

RAY
When it's happenin' like that, it's just right.

PAT
I know what you mean—I got the *shivers* in this studio tonight.

MARGIE
That's 'cause they ain't paid the heatin' bill.

RAY *(laughs)*
I got a question for all of you. . . how'd you like to go on the road with me.

Ethel and Pat squeal with delight. . . but Margie remains cool.

MARGIE
How much you gonna pay?

RAY *(beat)*
Ahmet takes care of all that stuff.

MARGIE
Ya mean he don't listen to you?

RAY *(beat)*
He does. . . Brother Ray'll take care of you, honey.

MARGIE
My mama taught me to take care of myself. . . honey.

RAY
Is your mother here?

MARGIE
No, she ain't. . . but I speak for us.

RAY
Okay, Miss Speak For Us, how about twenty dollars?

MARGIE *(playfully)*
Forty a week—each.

RAY
Forty each?!

The other Cookies voice their approval, egging Margie on.

RIGHT: Archival photo of Ray Charles recording at Atlantic Records during the early days of his association with the company. ABOVE: The scene was re-created for the movie.

What would please me is if people would say, "One thing about Ray's music, it's sincere. You may not like everything he does, but it's real. It's always genuine." If I got that kind of accolade for the rest of my career, or even after I'm dead, that would please me very much.

—Ray Charles

MARGIE
You heard me.

RAY
How 'bout twenty-five?

MARGIE
We'll take thirty.

RAY (beat)
I better say yeah. . . 'fore you talk me outta my drawers.

Ray holds his hand out to Margie.

RAY (cont'd)
Deal. . . ?

Margie shakes his hand. Gently, Ray FEELS HER WRIST. . .

RAY (CONT'D)
Margie, right? From now on. . . y'all's the Raelettes.

MARGIE
Does that mean we have to "Let Ray?"

RAY (laughs)
Lord. . . what am I gonna do with you?

Finally, Margie smiles.

MARGIE
You'll think of somethin'. . .

She gazes at Ray as he delicately caresses her wrist.

INT. ROYAL PEACOCK–DAY–1957
Jeff is hustling Fathead along, it's the beginning of rehearsal. Ethel introduces herself to Mary Ann.

RAY
This is what we're gonna do. . . From now on it's four-part harmony.

Mary Ann watches The Raelettes suspiciously as Ray coaches his new singers.

RAY (cont'd)
Ethel you sing alto, Margie the tenor, Pat, soprano. . . an' Mary Ann, bass.

MARY ANN
I ain't no bass. I'm a soprano.

MARGIE
I'll sing bass.

Mary Ann looks up at Margie, surprised.

MARGIE (cont'd)
Where I come from. . . we can sing anything.

MARY ANN
We're talkin' 'bout singin', sugar, not hog callin'.

Some of the band members start to laugh.

MARGIE
Who you callin' a hog. . . ?

MARY ANN
Well, if the corn cob fits. . .

MARGIE
You better shut your mouth. . .

All the guys in the band are on the floor laughing as Margie starts toward Mary Ann. Jeff jumps in between.

JEFF
Hold on, 'less I fine both y'all.

RAY
What's all the cacklin' about? Mary Ann, honey, I've written somethin' special for you. . . a solo.

MARY ANN
A solo. . . ?

RAY
Come down here so I can play it for you.

Mary Ann looks at Margie with a look of triumph as Ray begins to play the bluesy gospel intro to "What Kind of Man."

INT. SANDPIPER–NIGHT–1957

RAELETTES
What kind of man are you. . . ?

Mary Ann does a steamy rendition of "Man" before a packed house. Ray's lyrics foreshadow a painful story. . . .

MARY ANN & RAELETTES
Why do I love you so?
What kind of man are you. . .
when you don't love me no more?

INT. RAY'S HOTEL SUITE–DAY–1957

JEFF
Ethel, come here and see the new piano Ray got. It's called a Wurlitzer.

The band members crowd around Ray as he demonstrates his new Wurlitzer Electric Piano. It's Margie now, sitting with Ray at the piano. She brings him a drink. Rubs his shoulders affectionately. Mary Ann watches, suffering.

MARY ANN & RAELETTES (V.O.)
What kind of man are you?
I jes' can't satisfy, No matter how I try.

EXT. STREET OUTSIDE CIVIC HOTEL–DAY–1957- MUSIC CONTINUES
The Band members—including Mary Ann—gather around a strange vehicle, a Chevy Wagon chopped in the middle and extended to hold eight passengers plus equipment. The new band bus. . .

FATHEAD
Looks like a goddamn Weenie-Mobile.

The group cracks up. Something catches Mary Ann's eye: Down the alley, Jeff opens the door of a new '56 Caddie. . . for Ray and Margie.

THE OTHER FAMILY

You can't do a story about a musician without understanding his "other family"—his collaborators. Musicians speak a different language, the language of notes and rhythms that can only be understood by other musicians. To understand Ray Charles, we had to reveal not only his traditional relationships with wife, kids, girlfriends, and business partners, but also his experiences with his "other family," the musicians in his band.

We shot the film in New Orleans which is one of the great musical cities of the world. We used many wonderful New Orleans musicians recruited by local trumpeter Jamil Sharif but we also cast several wonderful actors who can play music. Terrence Howard who plays Gossie McKee, actually plays the guitar. Bokeen Woodbine who plays Fathead Newman, had learned the saxophone in school and worked hard to be able to blow the horn accurately in many sequences; and Chris Thomas King who plays Lowell Fulson, is a talented singer and blues guitarist. I'm very proud of the musical sequences in this film because they feature great musicians on stage.

—Taylor Hackford

MARY ANN & RAELETTES (V.O.)
What kind of man are you?
Why do you tell me lies. . . ?

Mary Ann glares at Ray. . . stricken.

INT. CIVIC HOTEL CORRIDOR–NIGHT–1957–
MUSIC CONTINUES
Elevator doors open. . . and a laughing Margie bursts into the hallway with Ray. She guides him to her room and they kiss, disappearing inside. PULL BACK to reveal Mary Ann at the end of the corridor, watching. After Ray and Margie stumble into her room, Mary Ann reaches for her suitcase and leaves.

MARY ANN (V.O.)
I wanna know, I wanna know,
I wanna know. . . Oh, oh, oh. . . about you.

EXT. STREET OUTSIDE CIVIC HOTEL–DAY–1957–
MUSIC CONTINUES
A taxi swerves to the curb and Mary Ann jumps out.

MARY ANN
Give me two seconds and we're going to the airport.

Mary Ann walks up to Ray's '56 Cadillac. . . snatches a loose brick from a planter. . . and hurls it through the windshield. She storms back to the cab, jumps in. . . and speeds away.

DISSOLVE TO:

INT. RAY'S BATHROOM–CIVIC HOTEL–DAY–1957
A syringe, spoon, and heroin capsules.

FATHEAD
Let's see what we got in the goodie bag. This stuff will fly you to the moon. Give me your hand. Here's three. Hold on, here's three more. . .

RAY
I thought you were my friend, the weight feels off, man.

Ray and Fathead are splitting up capsules of heroin.

FATHEAD
Don't start with me, Ray.

RAY
The weight is off.

FATHEAD
It ain't off. . .

RAY *(dawning on him)*
Man, you get high 'fore you go to cop, an' the dealers spank your ass! You gotta have more discipline.

FATHEAD
You know, man, I ain't messin' up my high tonight, sitting here, arguin' with you!

Fathead picks up his capsules and stomps out.

RAY *(calling after him)*
Hey, tie me off!

FATHEAD *(shouts back)*
Take care of your bad self, you know so much. . . Mr. Ray Charles. . .

Ray tries to put the heroin capsules on the sink and they fall to the floor.

RAY
Damn!

FLASHCUT TO BLACK:

INT. ROBINSON HOME–DAY–1937–FOURTH ARETHA DREAM
Aretha materializes out of the darkness, rising from her easy chair, but then she sees something that breaks her heart. She turns away, unable to look. . .

INT. RAY'S BATHROOM\BEDROOM–CIVIC HOTEL–
DAY–1957
. . . as Ray turns to the sound of the TV in the next room.

RAY
Margie, get in here!

MARGIE *(opening the door)*
What do ya want Ray?

RAY
Do me a favor, sweetheart, and pick those up.

Margie begins to pick up the fallen capsules.

RAY *(cont'd)*
You're gonna have to get me off.

Margie gives Ray a look, placing the capsules in his hand.

MARGIE
I'll do it if you let me try some. . .

RAY
This ain't for little girls.

MARGIE
I ain't no little girl.

RAY *(beat)*
Baby. . . junk'll take you places you don't wanna go.

MARGIE
Why do you do it, then?

RAY *(beat)*
It. . . it helps me create. I feel like I'm perfect when I do this.

MARGIE
See? I want to share that with you.

RAY *(intensely)*
Margie, listen to me. If I *ever* hear 'bout you messin' with dope. . . you're through. You better believe that more'n you believe in Jesus. . .

That stuns Margie. . . tears fill her eyes. She hesitates, studying Ray a moment.

MARGIE
Don't say that, baby. Y'know, I watch your show every night. . . but it's always new to me. Maybe 'cause it's new to you. You live every word of a song. . . then you bend some crazy note, an' damn if you don't break my heart. You got genius, Ray. . . *(tenderly)* . . . an' I just wanna be part of that.

That touches Ray. He leans over and kisses her deeply, forgetting the heroin. He spins her around, passionately kisses her neck, sliding her dress above her thighs. Margie closes her eyes and hears Fathead's sax wailing the sexy intro to "The Right Time."

INT. ATLANTIC RECORDING STUDIO–NIGHT–1958–MUSIC CONTINUES
Margie and Ray, totally absorbed in one another, sing "The Right Time". . . as the Raelettes back them up.

RAY
You know the night time. . .

MARGIE
Night and day. . .

RAY
Is the right time. . .

Continue song to:

THE RAELETTES
Night and day. . .

MARGIE
You know I love you. . .

THE RAELETTES
Night and day. . .

MARGIE
No one above you. . .

Ahmet, Tom, Jesse, and Jerry watch from the booth.

JESSE
Look at him. Look at his knees shaking, he's got that junkie itch. . . he's hooked.

JERRY
I know, but listen to that sound. He's brilliant.

JESSE
You can never trust a junkie, man.

JERRY
What do you want me to do. Listen to him, man.

Ahmet watches Ray jerk and scratch, deeply concerned.

DISSOLVE TO:

INT. RAY AND DELLA'S KITCHEN–DAY–1958–MUSIC CONTINUES
A FROSTED BIRTHDAY CAKE with three flickering candles.

DELLA
Okay. 1, 2, 3,. . . blow!

Ray, a PREGNANT Della, Jeff, and three-year-old Ray Jr. sit around the table. The little boy takes a mighty breath and blows.

MANAGER
It's in the contract, is what's wrong.

When Jeff runs up to Ray.

JEFF *(whispering urgently)*
Ray, you got twenty minutes left. . .

RAY
What do you want to do?

JEFF *(nods at the owner)*
That fool's gonna hold us to every second of this contract.

RAY
You go baby-sit him. I'll take care of it.

Jeff leaves.

RAY
Did he blow 'em out?

DELLA
Every one of them.

Ray applauds his son, delighted.

INT. A RENOVATED CLUB ALABAMA–NIGHT–1958
Ray and Margie finish "The Right Time," and the elegantly
dressed black crowd gives them a big hand. They want more.
Ray stands up, ready to walk off the stage.

RAY
Thank you very much. Please give a round of applause
for Margie Hendricks. Thank you, and good night.

In the audience, the manager shows Jeff a contract.

MANAGER
Hey, you wanna get paid?

JEFF
What's wrong?

RAY *(cont'd)*
They say we got a little more work to do. . .

FATHEAD
That was the last song in the book.

RAY
It's never the last song, Fathead. *(playing a catchy bass riff)* Look, band, I want you to lay in and follow me. Say as I say, do as I do. . . know where I'm goin'. . .

The drummer picks up on Ray's electric piano riff with his cymbal and the band falls into an up-tempo groove.

RAY *(cont'd)*
Hey, mama, don't you treat me wrong,
Come an' love ya daddy all night long. . .
hey, hey. . . What'd I say?

The audience loves it. People start dancing. . . .

RAY *(cont'd)*
See the girl with the diamond ring?
She knows how to shake that thang. . .
hey, hey. . . What'd I say?

A WOMAN gets up on a table top and starts shimmying, her spaghetti straps slipping off her shoulders.

RAY *(cont'd)*
Tell your mama, tell your pa,
I'm gonna send you back to Arkansas. . .
hey, hey. . . Baby, what'd I say?

As Ray finishes, the audience goes crazy. A woman grabs Jeff:

WOMAN
Where can I buy that record?

DANCE STYLES

We also took great care in re-creating the dances of this era. I put Vernel Bagneris, a wonderful dancer and choreographer, in charge of all the dance sequences and he delivered brilliantly. Vernel pointed out to me that when Ray first toured, it was before the age of TV when *American Bandstand* homogenized dance styles. Before *Bandstand*, each city had their own dance craze so, in our film, the dancers in each club are performing in entirely different styles.

—Taylor Hackford

LANDMARK MOMENTS

When Ray released "What'd I Say" in 1959, he *crossed over*. Up to that time, he'd played almost exclusively to black audiences, but suddenly he was embraced by white audiences which meant that the seating arrangements at his concerts changed dramatically. Whites were now in the front rows and blacks were relegated to the balcony. Ray couldn't see this, of course, but he heard the change immediately because the white kids were more respectful and *quiet*. Ray asked his manager why there wasn't the usual "call and response" from the audience, and was told about the segregated crowd. Although he didn't like this change, he went along with it because he'd been a child of Jim Crow segregation all his life and black entertainers made most of their income touring the South.

Then one day in 1962, when Ray arrived to play a gig at the Municipal Auditorium in Augusta City, Georgia, he was met by a group of young protesters shouting integration slogans and challenging him not to play this Jim Crow venue. He tried to explain that he had no choice, but the protesters argued passionately that someone had to be the first to stand up to Jim Crow. Why not Ray Charles?

Ray thought for a moment and then ordered his band back on the bus. The promoter threatened to sue but Ray would not be swayed. This decision cost him dearly. Not only was he sued by the promoter, the state of Georgia made an example of him by banning Ray from ever playing in the state again. Believe me, Ray Charles was a tough businessman and he loved money as much as anyone else. Georgia was Ray's highest-grossing state so he suffered major financial losses for this decision, but he stood by his decision and never played a Jim Crow show again.

I found this event particularly interesting because until that day, Ray had never been overtly political. Then suddenly, he took a stand and changed everything. He was the first major African-American performer who refused to play Jim Crow in the South and his actions helped turn the tide. Later, he became a major supporter of the integration movement and supported Martin Luther King financially, but this was the beginning, and we recreated this historic moment in the film.

—Taylor Hackford

JEFF
I don't know. . . It don't exist. . . But I'll tell Ray he should record it.

INT. ATLANTIC RECORDING STUDIO–NIGHT–1958–MUSIC CONTINUES
Ray, Ahmet, Jerry and Tom listen to the playback of "What'd I Say." We hear Ray's recorded voice doing a series of moans and groans which the Raelettes mimic, creating a sexy call and response.

RAY
I'm tellin' you man, that's outta sight, it's a hit.

JERRY
It's great. But what the hell do we do with this? It's too damn long.

RAY
Man, I've been playin' this every night on the road and it always brings down the house—guaranteed.

AHMET (motions to booth)
Tom, cut playback and come in here.

JERRY
Ray, you're probably right, I'm sure you're right. I've never heard a sound like it, but how do we market this to kids, it's got sex all over it. It's too damn sexual.

TOM
We could cut the second verse. . . pop into the chorus. . .

RAY
You cut that, I cut you in half.

TOM
We could split it up. Side A and Side B. It's been done before. . . what the hell.

AHMET
Do it. . .

RAY
Yeah, baby!!!

JERRY (getting excited)
We're Atlantic. We'll release in the summer. . . there's less censorship when school's out and kids are ready to kick loose. . .

Ahmet nods knowingly at Jerry, signaling him to exit.

JERRY (cont'd) (immediately understands)
Come on, Tom, let's split this pumpkin in two. . . show me some of this genius of yours.

Jerry and Tom Dowd leave Ahmet and Ray alone.

RAY (scratching and rocking)
A little on A and a little on B. . . damn Ahmet, that's outta sight, baby.

Ahmet and Ray share a laugh.

AHMET
How you feeling, Ray?

RAY
I'm feelin' groovy, baby.

AHMET (beat)
I'm talking about the junk. . . (off Ray's silence) It's showing. You're scratching all the time, you can't sit still.

RAY
Ahmet, have I ever missed a date?

AHMET
No, you never have. . . but. . .

RAY (cutting him off)
Can I deliver a record in one take?

AHMET
Ray, you deliver better than anyone I know. . . but I'm not talking to you as a businessman, I'm talking to you as a *friend*. I'm worried about you. And as a friend, I've got to tell you. . . your slip is hanging.

That makes Ray chuckle.

A MONSTER WITH FOOTPRINTS

One song or another is always topping the hit parade; many come and go and leave little trace behind. "What'd I Say" was a monster with footprints bigger than its numbers. Daringly different, wildly sexy, and fabulously danceable, the record riveted listeners. When "What'd I Say" came on the radio, some turned it off in disgust, but millions turned up the volume to blasting and sang, "Unnnh, unnnh, ooooh, ooooh" along with Ray and the Raelettes. "What'd I Say" became the life of a million parties, the spark of many romances, a song to date the summer by. For Ray, it was a breakthrough like "I Got a Woman" four years before, but much, much bigger. "What'd I Say" brought Ray Charles to everybody. In faraway Liverpool, Paul McCartney heard "What'd I Say" and chills went up and down his spine: "I knew right then and there I wanted to be involved in that kind of music." "What'd I Say" earned Ray his biggest royalties ever, raised his price on the road, and made a fortune for Atlantic, too, contributing mightily to the label's first-ever million-dollar month in gross sales.
—Michael Lydon, *Ray Charles*, 1998

RAY
My slip is hangin'. . . ? You been hangin' 'round us country boys too long. Don't worry 'bout me, baby. . . if the monkey gets heavy, I'll get me an organ grinder an' put 'im to work. Let's get this record out.

Ray laughs. Ahmet smiles but his concern deepens.

INT. ATLANTIC RECORDS RECORDING STUDIO–DAY–1959
Jerry enters and throws a BILLBOARD MAGAZINE onto Ahmet's desk.

EFX SHOT: *Billboard* headline spins into frame: "Ray Charles' Sexy 'What'd I Say': His Strongest Pop Record to Date."

INT. SHAW AGENCY (NEW YORK)–NIGHT–1959

MILT SHAW (V.O.)
He's off the Chitlin' Circuit—*Downbeat* just voted him Best Male Jazz Vocalist by a two-to-one margin. . . you wanna keep him in Philadelphia, you better find a bigger venue.

AS MILT SHOUTS INTO PHONE AND CIRCLES BILL BOARD CHART–EFX SHOT: Animated Billboard Pop Chart shows the song's upward progress from #82 to #43 to #26 to #15 to #6.

INT. SHAW AGENCY (NEW YORK)–DAY–STAGE–1959

MILT SHAW (*shouts into phone*)
Forget second billing. . . Ray Charles headlines at $1000 per or no deal! (*beat*) Terrific!

EXT. BEACH PARTY–DAY–2ND UNIT–L.A. LOCATION–1959
Jerry's prophesy comes true: white teenagers Watusi to "What'd I Say". . . total sexual liberation.

EXT. HOLLYWOOD FREEWAY–DAY–1959–VFX (STOCK)
Ray's new purple '59 Cadillac cruises down this famous LA freeway with the empty Weenie bringing up the rear.

DELLA (V.O.)
I'm havin' second thoughts 'bout this, Ray. I don't know anybody in L.A.

RAY (V.O.)
Bea, I don't want my kids growin' up in the South. L.A.'s where the Negro can spread his wings and fly.

DELLA (V.O.)
But my whole family's in Texas.

RAY (V.O.)
That's why we're movin' to L.A. . . .

EXT. RAY AND DELLA'S HEPBURN STREET HOME–DAY–1959
The purple Cadillac pulls up in front of Ray's new home. Jeff gets out, motions the Weenie Mobile forward. Ray and Della climb out of the Cadillac's back seat.

DELLA
Look at that big coconut tree.

RAY
That ain't no coconut tree, that's a palm tree.

He gives her a set of keys.

RAY (cont'd)
Here's the keys to your new life. (to Jeff) Watch the kids. I want to take Della in by myself.

AD LIBS from Jeff to Fathead in Weenie Mobile.

DELLA (overcome)
It's huge. . .

RAY
Wait till you see inside.

They walk up to the house.

INT. RAY AND DELLA'S HEPBURN STREET HOME–DAY–1959
Della and Ray enter. The place is exquisitely furnished.

DELLA
Oh, Ray. . . this is too much.

JERRY, AHMET, AND RAY

We never tried to impose a lot of phone calls on him. We talked once every few years. But I was very happy this time when he said, "Pardner"—he always called me that—"those were my best years, with you and Ahmet."

When people say, "You and Ahmet produced Ray Charles," put a big quotation mark around produced. We were attendants at a happening. My dear friend [writer] Stanley Booth once remarked, "When Ahmet and Jerry got ready to record Ray Charles, they went to the studio and turned the lights on. Ray didn't need them."
—Jerry Wexler, Rolling Stone, July 8-22, 2004

ABOVE: Richard Schiff as Jerry Wexler (left) and Curtis Armstrong as Ahmet Ertegun. BELOW: Jerry Wexler, circa 1950.

RAY
You should see the dining room.

He leads her toward. . . a CHRISTMAS TREE, decorated with ornaments. A mountain of toys and presents surrounds it.

DELLA *(puzzled)*
But it's October.

RAY
The band's on the road during the holidays,
so I figured we'd celebrate Christmas now.

DELLA
You're unbelievable. . .

Della gives Ray a big kiss as Jeff enters with Ray Jr. and his little brother, DAVID, a toddler.

DELLA *(cont'd)*
Kids, look what Santa brought! You must have been real good, 'cause it's so early.

Ray Jr. squeals with delight, making a beeline for the presents. The phone rings and Jeff answers it.

JEFF *(into phone)*
Hello. . . *(listens. . . troubled)* . . . how'd you get this number?

Della glances up. Jeff tries to mask his reaction.

JEFF *(cont'd)*
Ray. . . ?

RAY
Deal with it.

JEFF
Ray. . . it's important.

RAY
Who is it?

JEFF
It's Margie.

Ray takes the phone. Della sees the panic spread across Ray's face.

RAY *(into phone)*
Yeah?

Della goes to Jeff to get the baby.

DELLA *(takes Ray Jr.)*
C'mon Junior. . . help your mama change your brother's diaper.

RAY JR.
I want to play with my presents.

Della carries David and a whining Ray Jr. out of the room.

INT. HILTON HOTEL ROOM–DAY–1959
INTERCUT: MARGIE at the Hilton hotel room with Ray at his Hepburn house. Begin intro to "Believe to My Soul". . . .

MARGIE
(Surprise!) I flew out to surprise you.

Ray speaks with a quiet intensity, hoping Della doesn't hear.

RAY
Surprise me. . . ? Are you outta your mind? I'm here with my wife an' children!

MARGIE *(hurt)*
On the road. . . I'm Mrs. Ray Charles.

RAY
That's on the road.

MARGIE
Come on, baby. . . I got everything set up for us.

RAY
Didn't you hear what I said? We record in two weeks— I'll see you then.

He hangs up the phone. . . sensing he's got trouble.

INT. RAY AND DELLA'S HEPBURN STREET HOME– BEDROOM–DAY–1959–MOMENTS LATER–MUSIC CONTINUES
Della changes David's diaper. . . fighting back her emotions.

RAY (V.O.)
Need any help?

Della picks up David.

DELLA
No. . . all finished.

RAY
I'm gonna be here two weeks so we might as well celebrate Thanksgivin' an' Christmas! *(to Ray Jr.)* So come here and get these presents.

Ray Jr. runs to the tree and starts opening presents. Della walks up to Ray, holding David closer, trying to smile.

FADE TO BLACK:

INT. ATLANTIC RECORDS RECORDING STUDIO–NIGHT–1959

RAY *(singing)*
**One of these days, and it won't be long.
You're gonna look for me, and I'll be gone.**

Ray, at the Fender Rhodes, and the Raelettes—backed up by bass and drums—sing a lush, sensuous blues. . . "I Believe to My Soul."

RAELETTES
I believe, yes, I believe. . .

RAY
I believe right now.

RAELETTES
I believe, yes, I believe

RAY
I believe to my soul now, you're tryin' to make a fool out of me. . .

RAELETTES
I believe it, I believe it.

RAY (stops playing)
Hold it. . . three-part harmony's off. Let's take it from the top with the band.

THE HEALING GRACE OF MUSIC

It's hard to pick my favorite Ray Charles record. I love "Night Time Is the Right Time," "Unchain My Heart" and "What'd I Say" but my very favorite is "I Believe to My Soul," a slow, simple record that, in my opinion, captures the soul and sexiness of Ray Charles better than any other.

It's a hard choice because there are so many brilliant Ray Charles records. There's something healing in his music which became apparent while we were shooting.

We had a very tough shoot: The weather in New Orleans was very hot and humid and everyone was exhausted. I kept worrying that things were going to break apart but then we'd shoot another RC performance and everyone's spirits would lift. Instead of complaining about the long hours and back-breaking work, everyone was totally energized by the music.

—Taylor Hackford

As the Raelettes wait, Margie pours from a brown paper bag into a cup. Before Ray can count the band down, Tom Dowd—in the recording booth—plays back the Raelettes' track only. Ray is rocked.

RAY (cont'd)
Whoa, pardner. . . what's that?

Margie makes a face, mimicking Ray's, "Whoa, pardner." The other Raelettes giggle.

TOM (from the booth)
It's an eight track. . . just got it. We can record each part separately.

RAY
Whoa Nellie, I can't wait to see that.

Margie makes a face and apes Ray's, "Wow, baby."

RAY (cont'd) (hears Raelettes giggle)
What's so funny?

MARGIE
Nothin'. . . *pardner.*

RAY (beat)
Margie's drunk. . . Jeff. . . (off her silence) Go home. Sleep it off. . .

JEFF (approaching her)
C'mon, Marge, let me take you home.

MARGIE
I'll leave when I'm good an' goddamn ready!

RAY
She's good and goddamn ready now, Jeff.

MARGIE (to Ray)
Why don't you try an' make me leave, sucker?! Teach you to treat me like a piece of meat!

JEFF (gently taking her arm)
Margie, all this ain't necessary. . .

IN BOOTH

JERRY
Shall we step in?

AHMET
It's Ray's business. Leave it alone.

Margie flips Ray the bird and the other girls bust up. Ray's frustrated, he doesn't know what's happening. . .

RAY
Goddammit! All of y'all get the hell outta here—right now!

MARGIE
See. . . ? The cold bastard wouldn't walk 'cross the street to spit on you if your ass was on fire!

Ray escapes inside himself as Jeff herds the girls out the door. (ad libs on exit.) But the moment they're gone. . . he turns his attention back to business.

RAY
Okay, Tom, this is what I want you to do. We'll finish the band tracks, then lay my vocals and do the harmony part.

TOM
How are we gonna do the harmony, you sent the girls away?

> I've never written or arranged anything I was unhappy with later. I know that sounds boastful but I've got to be truthful.
>
> —Ray Charles, Liner notes,
> *The Genius of Soul Live!*

RAY
Don't worry 'bout it, baby. . . jes' play my voice for me and get me an "Oh Johnny" girl.

TOM (*starting tape playback*)
Alright, stand by for playback. (*to Ahmet*) What the hell's an "Oh Johnny" Girl?

AHMET
I got an idea. . .

INT. ATLANTIC RECORDS RECORDING STUDIO–NIGHT–1959
A YOUNG GIRL stands at the microphone.

Ray sings the last verse. She comes in with. . .

> YOUNG GIRL
> **Oh, Johnny. . .**

Ray finishes.

> RAY
> Tom, let's go back and record the harmonies and the overdubs.

Ray sings harmony.

> RAY *(cont'd) (singing falsetto)*
> **I believe, yes, I believe. . .**

IN A SERIES OF MATCHED DISSOLVES—
Ray sings three falsetto harmonies, each one feminine and distinctive. (ad libs inc: "Let's double it. . . let's triple it.")

INT. ATLANTIC RECORDS–RECORDING BOOTH–NIGHT–1959
Ahmet and Jerry hover over Tom at the controls, amazed at the flawless sound. . .

> TOM *(stunned)*
> Alright, Ray, it's rolling. . . I've seen overdubs, but this guy. . .

> AHMET
> . . . is Ray Charles.

> JERRY
> He's had the new contract for two months, let's take him out for a drink after and get him to sign it.

> AHMET
> No, Margie's put him in a bad mood. I'll call Milt and arrange to fly out and meet him on the road next week.

CUT TO:

INT. DETROIT THEATER–DRESSING ROOM–DAY–1959
Milt Shaw and Ray share a joint.

> ## Music is nothing separate from me. It is me. . . You'd have to remove the music surgically.
>
> —Ray Charles, liner notes, *The Genius of Soul Live!*

> MILT SHAW
> You're doing really well, Ray. They're going to up you to 15 per.

Jeff is directing the musicians.

> JEFF
> We rehearse in 10 minutes, guys.

> RAY *(to Jeff)*
> Could you get me some cigarettes from downstairs?

Jeff heads downstairs.

> MILT SHAW
> You know, your Atlantic contract expires in four months.

> RAY
> Yeah, I got the new one with me—they're doublin' my royalties.

> MILT SHAW *(pauses)*
> Listen, before we jump back into that pond, I thought I'd find out what else was out there. . . I had a very productive chat with ABC/Paramount.

> RAY
> ABC? Who said you could do that? You know good and well Atlantic's family, just like the Shaw Agency.

> MILT SHAW
> My job is to get you the best deal possible, and ABC's very interested.

Milt hesitates. . . waiting for Ray to take the bait.

RAY
How interested?

MILT SHAW
How about a $50,000 advance. . . each year for three
years. You produce your own records. They'll deduct
recording costs and give you 75 percent.

Ray and Jeff are stunned, but they remain silent.

MILT SHAW *(cont'd)*
Ahmet and Jerry are flying in tonight. . . will you put
them off so I can talk things out with ABC?

RAY
My mama always said, there ain't nothin' wrong
with talkin'.

Milt takes a long hit on the joint. . . and smiles.

INT. DETROIT THEATER–NIGHT–1959

We hear Ray's brass section blow "Let the Good Times Roll."

The house is packed, grooving. SUDDENLY, Ray waves his arms.

RAY
Cut! Cut! *(turning to the audience)* I wanna apologize to
you folks. You paid good money to hear us tonight. . .
an' my horn section keeps blowin' it—and that ain't no

joke. Ain't that right, Trumpet #3. *(off the audience's laughter)* We're gonna start again an' get it right. Can we get it right?

A trumpet player, PAUL—black, late 20s—glares at Ray as he counts them off.

TIME LAPSE DISSOLVE TO:

INT. DETROIT THEATER–BACKSTAGE–NIGHT–1959
The announcer shouts to a cheering audience: "Let's Hear it for the High Priest, Ray Charles." Jeff leads Ray off stage as the curtain drops down behind them.

RAY
The band was pretty good but I need to talk to Paul.

JEFF
Here?

RAY
Yeah.

JEFF
Paul, come here. *(to Ray)* What's goin' on?

RAY
I gotta talk to him.

Paul, the black trumpet player, walks over.

PAUL *(playing it cool)*
Yeah, Jeff, what's shakin'?

RAY
What's shakin'?! I told you not to get onstage when you're *high*—that's what's shakin'! Take your things an' get your ass outta here. . . you're fired!

Ray grabs Jeff's arm and storms off, but Paul follows them.

PAUL
This ain't fair. . . you get high!

RAY
You ever heard me come on stage like that?! I *handle* my business. I don't let what I do off-stage affect me on stage.

PAUL *(absorbing that)*
Ray. . . gimme a break, man. I got a family.

RAY
You think I don't? Get out. . .

He walks off. . . and Paul realizes it's over.

PAUL *(shouts)*
Go to hell. . . ya goddamn hypocrite! You ain't human, Ray.

That hits Ray. . . but he doesn't even break stride.

RAY *(coldly, to Jeff)*
I shouldn't have to deal with this, Jeff. You should've caught that.

JEFF
You ain't makin' it any easier. Man, your drawers are raggedy. . .

RAY
What'd you say to me?

JEFF
You heard me! You got different rules for yourself. . .
an' Fathead an' Margie, too! Every night, I see a
couple of hop heads an' a drunk out there. . .
(trying to calm himself) Yeah. . . I finally said it.
So if you wanna fire me, too. . . go 'head.

RAY *(a long pause)*
Do your job, man. Pay him off an' get 'im the
hell outta here.

INT. DETROIT THEATER–BACKSTAGE (SIMULTANEOUS) 1959

MILT
Ray. . . Ahmet and Jerry stopped by to say hello.

Ahmet and Jerry walk up, escorted by Milt.

AHMET
Great show. . . how about some dinner?

RAY
Sorry, Ahmet. . . I gotta fly out to Cleveland tonight, do
a TV show. *(feigning anger)* Milt, why didn't you tell me
they were here?

MILT SHAW *(playing along)*
Sorry, Ray. . . I thought you were free.

AHMET
No sweat. . . we'll do it another time. By the way,
Nesuhi finally came up with the title for your new
LP: *The Genius of Ray Charles*. . . like it?

RAY *(humbled)*
Hard not to like.

AHMET
It's the truth, my friend.

RAY
I apologize. I gotta make this show. It came up

at the last minute. They bought me a plane ticket
and everything.

AHMET
Call me when your schedule opens up. Or I can always
fly to New Orleans. We'll eat at Dukey Chase's. . .

RAY
Alright, I'll call you.

Jeff leads Ray off, leaving Milt, Jerry, and Ahmet.

MILT SHAW
I'm sorry, guys. . . he agreed to this TV thing
without telling me. It wasn't on the schedule.
(waving at the manager) Listen, I gotta settle up
with the house. . . if you want to meet for a late
dinner, I'll be free around one.

I'VE NEVER SEEN EARS LIKE THIS!

For *The Genius of Ray Charles* sessions I had the entire Count Basie band without Count Basie, seven of my favorites from the Duke Ellington Band and I had Quincy Jones do the arrangements. All of these famous musicians were not entirely sure that this blind piano player, who was the star, really deserved all of this. They were kind of looking down their noses a bit, making little wisecracks, and I could see that the atmosphere was not too cool. Ray called me over and said, "The fourth bar, the third trumpet player, there's a bad note." I said, "Are you sure?" He said, "I'm telling you there's a bad note." So I called Quincy over and he said, "Impossible. I didn't hear it." I said, "Well, there's only one thing to do, have the trumpets play one by one." So they each played, and sure enough, the third trumpet player was hitting a wrong note. Quincy was astonished. He said, "I've never seen ears like this!" The whole band applauded and it changed the session, saved it—from then on they worked like they never had before.

—Nesuhi Ertegun, as quoted in
What'd I Say, by Ahmet Ertegun

As Milt scurries off, Jerry gives Ahmet a look.

> JERRY
> That little bastard's up to something. Have you heard anything. . . ?

> AHMET
> Relax, will you? Ray will sign. . . Atlantic's family.

Jerry stares after Ray. . . unconvinced.

CUT TO:

INT. SAM CLARK'S SUITE–ABC-PARAMOUNT
RECORDS–NYC–DAY–1959
SAM CLARK—a balding impresario, mid 50s—and his ABC
Records execs surround Ray, Milt, and Jeff.

> SAM CLARK
> Enough formalities. Let's go into the office, Ray.
> I hope I can call you Ray. I want you to feel
> comfortable here because at ABC things are going
> to be better for you. When you move from an indie
> label to a major it will mean that you'll sell a lot
> more records, as well as draw bigger crowds. . .
> white and Negro.

> RAY
> But I've been with Atlantic for a lot of years. I'd like
> to give 'em a chance to match your offer.

> SAM CLARK
> Certainly, but I doubt they'll be able to. Remember
> we're giving you a state-of-the-art deal.

> RAY
> I appreciate that, Mr. Clark, but I been thinkin',
> since I'm producin' my records, I should own
> the masters.

Everyone's jaw drops, including Jeff and Milt Shaw.

> SAM CLARK
> Mr. Charles. . . we've never done that before, no record
> company has. . .

THE GENIUS HITS THE ROAD

That winter [of 1960] Elvis came back from the army and John F. Kennedy started running for president. *Billboard* reported that in 1959 albums had outsold singles for the first time, 6 million to 4.75 million, and Ray put weeks into planning his first album for ABC-Paramount. *Genius* and the jazz albums had balanced ballads and up-tempo tunes, but otherwise had been arranged in no particular way. Ray wanted to give this album a theme, and he came up with a simple one: place songs. Soon he had a list, "Moonlight in Vermont," "Alabamy Bound," "California, Here I Come," and others in the same vein. Riding in the Caddy, he often broke into Hoagy Carmichael's "Georgia on My Mind." One day his driver said, "Why don't you record that?" and "Georgia" got added to this list.
—Michael Lydon, *Ray Charles,* 1998

> RAY
> I think I have to have it that way in order to
> leave Atlantic.

Clark looks around at his executives. . . they're sweating. . .
they've let the rabbit into the briar patch.

INT. ATLANTIC RECORDS OFFICES–DAY–1960
Ahmet and Jeff sit calmly while Jerry explodes at Ray.

> JERRY
> Ahmet wouldn't believe it. You know why Ray?!
> Because it's unbelievable. Unbelievable! Ahmet
> believes that we're a family here at Atlantic. I
> believe that we're a family here at Atlantic.
> Obviously, you don't!

Ray sits quietly, listening to Jerry's tirade.

> JERRY *(cont'd)*
> What are you doing, Ray? What the hell are
> you doing? You're selling yourself to a soulless,
> white bread organization that doesn't give a damn
> about Negro music! *(dripping with sarcasm)* Sam

143

THE BUSINESS OF RAY CHARLES

Everyone knows that Ray Charles was a brilliant artist but in our film, you also discover that he was a consummate businessman. Ray learned at the feet of two of America's greatest music executives, Ahmet Ertegun and Jerry Wexler, who nurtured Ray's great talent. However, after many years of success, Ray left Atlantic for a deal with a major label, ABC-Paramount. Why did he leave? Because he negotiated a deal that was unprecedented in the recording industry. Not only did ABC let him produce his own records and keep 75 percent of the profits, they also gave him ownership of his master recordings which no one, not even Frank Sinatra, had managed to negotiate.

I wanted people to understand that Ray Charles broke the ground for other artists. Here was a black man, a blind man, who raised the bar for everyone else: The Beatles, Bob Dylan, the Rolling Stones, Bruce Springsteen, Michael Jackson, and all these great artists who came afterwards built their deals on what Ray Charles negotiated.

—Taylor Hackford

Clark's a front man, that's rich. Sam Clark is a corporate slug who wouldn't know the difference between Earl Hines and Art Tatum! We let you grow here, Ray. Nobody's taking credit for your talent, but we nourished it and let you do your thing. And, goddammit, we deserve better than this!

RAY
Look here Jerry, don't think I don't 'preciate what you guys've done. Ahmet, I'll always be proud of the work we did together. But Atlantic's done pretty good money-wise on my records. . . right?

AHMET
Yes, Ray, we've done very well.

RAY
Well, you guys are the ones that taught me makin' records is a business, an' to make the best deal they can. Seventy-five cents out of every dollar, an' ownin' my own masters is a damn good deal. . . can you match it?

144

AHMET
We'd love to match it, Ray, but we just can't. . .
that's a better deal than Sinatra's got. . . I'm very
proud of you.

Ray laughs, clasping his hand over Ahmet's. A bittersweet
moment for Ahmet. . . Jerry storms out.

AHMET (cont'd)
. . . I guess those boys got a taste of country dumb.

INT. ABC RECORDING STUDIO–NIGHT–1960
We hear music from another place, another time. . . the lush,
string arrangement of "Georgia on My Mind." A sound totally different from anything Ray's done before. . . A symphon-
ic string section and choir surround Ray at the piano. Their

music is mainstream Pop. . . until Ray starts to sing and colors it Blue.

**INT. ABC RECORDING STUDIO–GREEN
ROOM–NIGHT–1960–CONTINUOUS**
Isolated from the action, Fathead and Margie confront Jeff.

MARGIE
Listen to that crap. . . I thought ABC wasn't gonna force
nothin' on 'im.

JEFF
They didn't. It was Ray's idea. . . somethin' new.

MARGIE (beat)
What're we then, Jeff? Somethin' ole. . . ?

FATHEAD
Yeah, what 'bout us? We gotta eat, too. . .

Jeff shrugs it off as Margie turns away. . . listening to the music. Despite herself, it moves her. She slips a flask from her purse. . .

CUT TO:

INT. AMERICAN BANDSTAND STUDIO–DAY–1960–STOCK
Dick Clark on a TV screen announces *American Bandstand's* hits.

DICK CLARK
And remaining at number one for the third straight week. . . is "Georgia on My Mind"—Ray Charles' first record to top the charts.

INT. RAY AND DELLA'S HEPBURN STREET HOME/BED-ROOM–DAY–1960
Little David plays in his playpen in his room across the hall. Ray Jr. is watching Dick Clark on TV.

RAY JR.
My daddy's number one.

Della enters.

DELLA
Where's your daddy?

RAY JR. *(pointing)*
In the bathroom.

Della hesitates a moment. . . then knocks on the bathroom door.

DELLA
Ray. . . ? Jeff's on his way.

Ray comes out, wearing trousers and a T-shirt. He's humming a tune, scratching his ear. Della watches suspiciously as he carries out a small container.

DELLA *(cont'd)*
What's that?

RAY *(opening shaving kit)*
My new shaver.

Ray lays the kit in his suitcase. He feels his clothes.

RAY (CONT'D)
Brown pants on top of the blue.

Ray Jr. watches, fascinated.

RAY JR.
Daddy, if you can't see. . . how do you choose the right colored socks?

RAY
C'mere, boy, I'll show you something. *(rolling down his sock)* See that "two" in there? I have that number sewed in real thick, so I can feel it—two's brown, one's black, an' three's blue. Four, where are you. . .

DRESSING RAY

Minimizing variables had long been a principal way Ray overcame his handicap and coped with his complex life. For example: a small room at RPM served as Ray's wardrobe room. Along one wall stood drawers for socks and underwear; from bars along three walls hung Ray's outfits. Each hanger held a matched jacket, slacks, and shirt combination, ranging from quiet daywear to gaudy brocade tuxedos for the stage. Every hanger had a number: the brown, beige, and green outfits odd numbers; the grays, blacks, and blues even numbers. Beneath the clothes were dozens of pairs of shoes, most made by Bally, in long neat rows; the brown shoes had a straight line scratched on the sole under the instep, the black shoes had a cross. The system had been in place for over thirty years. By simply telling his valet, "Bring me number eight," and running his finger over his shoe sole, Ray could be sure, sight unseen, that he was wearing appropriate clothes in coordinated colors.

—Michael Lydon, *Ray Charles*, 1998

Ray is jittery, kinetic. . . high.

RAY JR.
Daddy. . . you're real happy, huh?

RAY
Yeah, son. . . I'm always happy.

DELLA *(beat)*
Junior. . . go downstairs an' let us know when Jeff's here.

RAY JR.
Sure, Mama.

Ray Jr. scampers out the door. Della looks at Ray. . .

DELLA
You're high. . . ain't ya?

RAY *(forcing a laugh)*
What's a church girl like you know 'bout gettin' high?

DELLA
Ray, answer my question.

RAY *(beat)*
Hey. . . I'm just feelin' good.

Della knows he's lying. We HEAR a car horn outside.

RAY JR. (O.S.)
Daddy, Jeff's here!

RAY
I'll call you when I get to Newport.

Ray grabs his suitcase and walks out.

RAY JR.
I'll help you, Daddy.

RAY
You gonna help your daddy down the stairs?
Alright, then.

Ray takes a smiling Ray Jr.'s hand. Ray Jr. looks very proud as he leads his father down the stairs. Della watches.

EXT. NEWPORT JAZZ FESTIVAL (STOCK SHOT)–DAY–1961

INT. BACKSTAGE TENT–NEWPORT JAZZ FESTIVAL–DAY– 1961
Ray and a DOWNBEAT REPORTER sit in folding chairs. Musicians and hangers-on mill around in the background.

RAY
It's a hit record. What the hell's wrong with that?

DOWNBEAT REPORTER
If it sells, it ain't jazz. Some critics are saying you've gone middle-of-the-road. The orchestra, the choir. . . the Perry Como Show.

That troubles Ray. . . but he shrugs it off.

RAY
Critics criticize. That's the root of the word. If I'm feeling the music, baby. . . it's real.

A MAN'S VOICE (O.S.)
No, it ain't. Ray Charles is a sell-out. He's the blind Liberace, leavin' those Rockin' Chair roots behind. . .

Ray laughs, recognizing the voice: It's Quincy's, all grown up.

RAY
Q. . . !

QUINCY
6-9!

The two friends embrace.

RAY (to the Reporter)
Baby, this interview's over.

The reporter trudges out of the room. The friends greet each other.

RAY (cont'd)
Can you believe that? These fools sayin' I can't do it no more?

QUINCY
So crank out another hit.

RAY
It ain't so easy to keep on bein' greasy, Q. . . where'd you blow in from?

QUINCY
Paris. France is where it's at, man.

RAY
That's what I hear. An' the sounds you been layin' down? Outta sight. . .

QUINCY
Y'know, we oughta record somethin' together. People will dig it. Where you goin' after the Festival?

RAY
D.C., Richmond, New Orleans, Georgia. . .
(a weary laugh) You know the game. Make a record, then get your ass out an' sell it.

QUINCY
Yeah, but down South? Man, I can't do that no more.

RAY *(beat)*
Why, Q? That's where the money is.

QUINCY
When I left Seattle an' went down there with Hamp. . . it was like I walked into a prison cell. A black man's a "boy" in Mississippi—even if he's 80 years old.

RAY *(laughing)*
Those crackers scared you, huh?

QUINCY
You were raised there. . . but I can't put up with it. Especially after livin' in Europe. I won't ever play Jim Crow again. . .

RAY *(shrugs)*
If you say so, Q. . .

QUINCY
No, I'm serious, Ray.

RAY *(laughs, trying to cover)*
Fine, baby, you're jes' leavin' more money on the table.

Despite Ray's bravado, Quincy's words weigh on him. . .

INT. RAY'S SUITE–THERESA HOTEL (HARLEM)–NIGHT–1961
Ray sits behind the Fender Rhodes, moody. . . still affected by Quincy's words. A haggard Margie lies on the bed.

RAY
You ready to work?

MARGIE
Work on what?

RAY
Get over here, you gotta help me with this one. Percy just gave me some new music.

Margie gets up slowly. . . then suddenly rushes into the bathroom. Ray hears the SOUND of her vomiting, and turns away, disgusted. After a moment, Margie steps out of the bathroom, embarrassed. . . wiping her face with a washcloth. Ray is silent for a moment. Then. . .

RAY *(cont'd) (wearily)*
Ya know. . . they're sayin' about me. . . . that I lost somethin'. That I've gone "middle-of-the-road." They may as well say the same thing 'bout you. You were the soul of this band. Now every time I turn around you're drunk. *(a sad laugh)* The drunk soul of a blind junkie. What a lovely couple. . . .
(off her silence) Why don't you just get outta here?

Margie stares at him for a long moment. Tears fill her eyes.

MARGIE
I ain't drunk, Ray. I'm pregnant. . . . *(off his stunned silence)* That's right. . . I'm havin' your baby.

RAY
Margie. . . you can't do that. We can talk to a doctor—

She SLAPS Ray. He just takes it.

MARGIE *(crying)*
What—I ain't your precious Bea. . . so I ain't good enough to have your baby?

Ray says nothing. . . and Margie's tears turn to rage.

MARGIE *(cont'd)*
You lay up in my bed every night, my bed! I'm gonna have this baby, Ray!

Ray gets up and tries to put his arms around her.

RAY
Alright. . . alright.

Ray tries to take her hand, but she steps back.

RAY *(cont'd)*
Margie. . . I love you. . . I'll pay for everything.

MARGIE *(simmering)*
No. . . it's gonna cost you a more than money. I want you to leave her. . . I want you to be with our baby.

RAY
You outta your goddamn mind? You knew the rules when we got into this. I ain't leavin' my damn family.

MARGIE *(a bitter laugh)*
You're a damn fool, you know that? 'Tween the dope an' the music an' me, you already done left your damn family. Sad part about it is. . . you don't even know it. *(stone cold)* From now on, it's strictly business 'tween us. Let's work. I need the money. . .

Margie snatches a lyric sheet off the piano. She waits, glaring at Ray. He hesitates, filled with conflicting emotions.

RAY
Use it, Margie. Use that anger.

He begins to play. His style is rough, hard. . . growing in intensity as he takes out his frustrations on the keyboard. This is streetfightin' music. . . and Margie's body begins to respond, moving to its rhythm. They both sing "Hit the Road Jack."

INT. THE BLUE ROOM–NIGHT–MUSIC CONTINUES–1961
The place is packed. . . and Margie is using it as Ray plays. She's at her sassy best, with the Raelettes backing her up.

> **MARGIE & RAELETTES**
> Hit the road, Jack, and don'tcha
> come back no more, no more. . .
> Hit the road, Jack, and don'tcha
> come back no more.

> **RAY**
> What ch'you say.

> **MARGIE & RAELETTES**
> Hit the road, Jack, and don'tcha
> come back no more, no more. . .
> Hit the road, Jack, and don'tcha
> come back no more.

> **RAY**
> Now, baby, listen baby,
> Don't you treat me this a'way 'cause
> I'll be back on my feet someday.

> **MARGIE**
> Don't care if you do 'cause it's understood,
> You ain't got no money,
> You just ain't no good.

> **RAY**
> Well, I guess if you say so,
> I'll have to pack my things and go.

> **MARGIE & RAELETTES**
> That's right! Hit the road, Jack. . .

The song takes on a special meaning for Ray and Margie. . . .

INT. SAM CLARK'S ABC OFFICE–DAY–MUSIC CONTINUES–1961
Sam Clark is ecstatic. . .

> **SAM CLARK** (*shouting into the phone*)
> Ray, it's Sam, can you hear me?—"Hit The Road" is our second number one! ABC's taking ads in all the trades. And congrats on the Grammy nomination! I *know* you're gonna win! Are you alright?

INT. RAY'S ROOM–THERESA HOTEL–DAY–1961
Ray lies on the couch, talking on the phone to Sam. He's slurring his words. . . stoned. In the background, Margie packs her suitcase. She closes it and walks up to Ray

> **RAY** (*into phone*)
> That's great, Sam. . . thanks. Yeah. . . bye.

He hangs up. Margie looks down at him.

MARGIE
I'll stop by Jeff's room an' get my money on the way out.

RAY
Margie. . . you don't have to leave.

MARGIE
I'm on your hit record. If I'm ever goin' solo. . . now's the time.

RAY
I don't want you to go.

MARGIE
For once. . . I'm doin' what's right for me.

She waits for a response, but Ray is silent. Margie steels her-self. . . then heads for the door.

RAY
Remember. . . the hummin'bird, right?

MARGIE *(confused)*
What. . . ?

RAY
The hummin'bird, Bea. . .

Bea. The name brings tears to Margie's eyes. She turns on her heel and strides out the door, slamming it behind her.

FLASHCUT TO BLACK:

INT. ROBINSON HOUSE–DAY–FIFTH ARETHA DREAM–1935
We're enveloped in RAY'S BLINDNESS again, his breath the only sound. In a moment, Aretha appears in the void. . . setting a place for someone at an old kitchen table. She doesn't look at us this time, she's lost in her own world. A little boy appears, sauntering toward the table. It's Ray's little brother, George.

CUT BACK TO:

INT. RAY'S ROOM–THERESA HOTEL–DAY–1961
Ray falls off the couch. He's terrified by the dream. . . He fumbles his way back up.

EXT. AUGUSTA CIVIC AUDITORIUM–DAY–1961
PAN A SEA OF PROTEST SIGNS READING: "NO MORE SEG-
REGATED SHOWS," "EQUAL RIGHTS FOR NEGROS IN GEOR-
GIA," "BOYCOTT JIM CROW." WIDEN to reveal. . .

Dozens of BLACK STUDENTS brandishing protest signs,
chanting. . . slowing the progress of Ray's tour bus as it inch-
es through the crowd. Finally, the bus comes to a stop. Jeff
leads Ray down the steps. A phalanx of cops plows through
the crowd, running interference for a WHITE PROMOTER. He
scrambles up to Ray. . .

WHITE PROMOTER
Ray. . . I'm sorry about this! You and your boys just
hurry inside. . . there's refreshments waitin'.

STUDENT PROTESTER (*pushing against the cops*)
Mr. Charles, did you know tonight's show is segregated?
The dance floor is "whites only". . . Negroes can't leave
the balcony.

That bothers Ray. . . but he shrugs it off.

RAY
That's the way it is here. This is Georgia.

STUDENT PROTESTER
You think we don't know that? Negroes are persecuted in
this state every day.

RAY
Ain't a damn thing I can do 'bout it. . . I'm just an
entertainer. We all gotta play Jim Crow down here.

WHITE PROMOTER
That's right, boy, get outta here. . .

STUDENT PROTESTER
It doesn't have to be that way, Mr. Charles.
You could be the first to change things right
here and now.

RAY (*moving on*)
I can't help ya, son. . .

WHITE PROMOTER
You heard him, boy! Now take this black trash and get your black asses on outta here!

The promoter takes Ray's arm to hustle him off. . . but he bristles, pulling away.

RAY
Jeff. . . ! Get 'em on the bus.

JEFF
You sure?

RAY
Get 'em on the bus.

WHITE PROMOTER
What?!

Jeff smiles, relishing the moment.

JEFF
Y'all heard 'im! Back on the bus!

The band members turn around, heading for the bus. The protesters begin to cheer. . .

WHITE PROMOTER
Ray. . . you can't be serious! What the hell is this?!

Ad libs as Jeff leads Ray toward the bus, the promoter at their heels.

They could segregate everything else, but they couldn't segregate the radio dial.

—Ahmet Ertegun, *What'd I Say*

WHITE PROMOTER *(cont'd)*
Ray, you know me. I ain't gonna' lose money 'cause you suddenly found religion. You got a contract—break it, I'll sue you and win.

As Ray and Jeff approach the bus.

WHITE PROMOTER *(cont'd)*
You'll never play Georgia again!

The student reaches through the cops. . . touching Ray as he strides by.

STUDENT PROTESTER
Thank you, Mr. Charles.

EXT. RAY'S TOURING BUS–DAY–1961
Ray and the band head for the bus bus as they converge on him, shaking his hand, slapping his back. Fathead gives him a hug. . . .

FATHEAD
That was righteous, man. . . 'bout time we did somethin'.

JEFF
I'm proud of you, boss. . . .

Jeff leads Ray to his seat, sitting next to him as the bus drives off. . . and the crowd's cheers fade into the distance. Ray rides along for a moment, silent. . . pensive.

RAY
Did ya hear about Margie, Jeff. . . ?

JEFF
What about her?

RAY
She's playing in Houston, Texas.

JEFF *(beat)*
Let her go, Ray. Let her go. . . .

In the background, an alto sax begins to rock. . . and we hear Ray's voice cry out, "UNCHAIN MY HEART!"

The other cop opens the door and several reporters and photographers surge into the room, flashing pictures and inundating Ray with questions. He coils back into his chair. . . humiliated.

Suddenly, the SOUND is sucked out of the room. . . and we watch in silence as the reporters assault Ray with their accusations. Then, Ray's voice cries out, painfully singing "You Don't Know Me" to the accompaniment of a lone piano. The poignant song underscores this blind man's torment.

> RAY (V.O.)
> You give your hand to me,
> And then you say hello,
> And I can hardly speak,
> My heart is beating so,
> And anyone could tell,
>
> You think you know me well,
> But you don't know me. . . .

A camera flashbulb whites out the screen. Burn through the whiteness to. . .

Archival photo of Ray Charles (below) being questioned by the Indianapolis police in November 1961 after his arrest on a drug charge. The scene was re-created in the movie to have the same feeling of foreboding.

**INT. RAY AND DELLA'S HEPBURN STREET HOME–DAY– 1961–
MUSIC CONTINUES**

The shades are drawn in Ray's darkened living room. He sits
alone, playing the piano as he sings:

> **RAY**
> You give your hand to me,
> And then you say hello,
> And I can hardly speak,
> My heart is beating so.
> And anyone can tell,
> You think you know me well,
> But you, you don't know me, no.
>
> Hi Baby. . .

Little David enters the room silently, watching his father.
After a moment, Della appears. She takes David's hand, hustles him to the door. Ray continues to play, turns to her:

> **RAY** *(cont'd) (quietly)*
> He can stay, Bea. . .

But David walks out the door. Bea starts to follow him out.

> **RAY** *(cont'd)*
> Bea. . . ?

Bea stops, turns.

> **RAY** *(cont'd)*
> Since I got back. . .

> **DELLA**
> Since you got out.

> **RAY**
> Yeah. *(beat)* Since I got here you haven't said
> two words to me. . .

> **DELLA**
> Ray. . . what am I gonna say? My words don't mean
> much to you anymore. Maybe they never did. . .

> **RAY**
> C'mon, Bea. You know I love you. . .

> **DELLA** *(beat)*
> You gonna stop, then. . . ?

> **RAY**
> Bea. . . you don't understand, there is a lot
> of hate out there.

DELLA *(bitterly)*
Yeah. . . *(beat)* I had to keep Junior home from school today. . . 'cause of what the other kids are sayin'.

That troubles Ray. . . deeply.

RAY
Those mean-spirited kids around here. . . We need to move to Beverly Hills. . .

DELLA
No, we're not. It's not where we live, Ray. . . it's what you're doin' to yourself! Those boys worship you. You want 'em to end up usin' that poison, too?

RAY
Bea, that's not fair.

DELLA
What's not fair. . .

The phone rings. He turns to it gratefully:

RAY *(into phone)*
Hello. . . ?

Ray listens for a moment. . . and he begins to smile.

RAY *(cont'd)*
Don't jive me, Milt. . . that's great! Tell ABC thank you and Sam, too.

Ray slams down the receiver, grabs Della, picks her up and twirls her around, laughing.

RAY *(cont'd)*
You're not going to believe this.

She pulls free.

DELLA
What happened?

RAY
ABC's lawyers got the case dropped! The police didn't have a warrant. . . !

DELLA'S OUTFITS

We dressed Della a little like a fifties housewife. She is very sweet and innocent and, in the beginning, she wears a lot of pastels—pinks and baby blues. She hardly ever goes out and she is pregnant in many of her scenes so we put her in an apron or bathrobe. Then, in the sixties, after Ray has become a huge success, her clothes are more expensive with nice jewelry, but they are always simple and tailored. I figured she is now shopping at Magnin; her clothes are slick but never gaudy.
—Sharen Davis, costume designer

DELLA *(relieved; troubled)*
They bought 'em off. . . .

RAY *(studying her)*
Dammit Bea. You want me to go to prison?

DELLA
No, I want you to stop lyin' to yourself, Ray. . . and they just made that completely impossible.

RAY
Bea, you don't understand.

DELLA
Make me (help me) understand?

Ray hesitates a moment, searching for the right words.

RAY
When I step out that door I'm all alone in the dark. Trying to do something that ain't no one ever done before in the music and the business. But I can't do it if I'm alone everywhere I go. I don't want to be alone in my own house, Bea. If you don't understand me. . . who will?

Baby David cries out from the living room.

DELLA *(conflicted)*
I don't know, Ray. . . I don't know.

Della runs into the living room. Ray turns back to the piano and again begins playing "You Don't Know Me."

RAY
I never knew the art of making love
Though my heart aches with love for you.
I can't deny. . .

As he sings, a single FLAME bursts from the piano top. . . and A SPOONFUL OF HEROIN appears, hovering over it. An apparition of Aretha materializes, her eyes burning with disapproval. Ray's voice trembles with passion now. . . as he walks an emotional tightrope between his cruel mistress and his reproachful mother.

SAM CLARK (V.O.)
COUNTRY MUSIC???

INT. SAM CLARK'S OFFICE–ABC–RECORDS–DAY–1961

SAM CLARK
COUNTRY MUSIC???

Sam Clark and his executives square off with Milt Shaw, Jeff and Ray.

RAY
That's right, Sam. . . .I've been singing country all my life. *(smiling fondly)* Hell, I played with the Florida Playboys.

SAM CLARK *(simmering)*
Ray, we've made a big investment in you and it's paying off handsomely . . . for both of us I might add. We don't want to lose your fan base.

RAY
Well, you got a point there. Only, I think we have more to gain than to lose.

SAM CLARK
(putting his foot down)
Ray, it's a bad idea. . .

RAY *(deadpan)*
Sam, when I came to ABC, you put it in my contract that I could choose my own music. . . would you like to read that paragraph?

Sam looks at Milt Shaw. . . Ray's got them again.

RAY *(cont'd)*
Trust me, Sam. I know what I'm doing.

FADE-UP INSTRUMENTAL INTRO TO
"ROCKHOUSE" AS WE CUT TO:

CLOSE-UP: JOE ADAMS—A pencil-thin mustache, elegant links on french cuffs, gold ring–purrs into the microphone: 1962

JOE ADAMS
Hellloooo Cleveland, it's time for THE MAIN ATTRAC-
TION. . . THE INNOVATOR OF SOUL, THE GENIUS
HIMSELF: RAAAY CHAAARLEZ.

INT. LARGE CLEVELAND THEATRE–NIGHT–1962
Jeff leads Ray on stage to thunderous applause. As Jeff seats
Ray at the piano, people start shouting out requests.

RAY
First of all, I wanna say thank you. . . How y'all
doin' tonight. . . ? *(a loud, rowdy response)* . . . a lot
of y'all might not know it, but I grew up in the
South, an' down there when you turn on the radio,
you always hear the Grand Ole Opry. . . That's the
music I grew up singin', so tonight I wanna give
y'all a little taste of my country roots.

The audience continues to be loud and sassy, shouting out
requests for "What'd I Say" and "Hit the Road Jack." Ray and
the Raelettes start singing to a noisy audience.

RAELETTES
I can't stop loving you. . .

JOE ADAMS
The lights up top, the ones in the mezzanine. Let's take
everything down and hit Ray with a follow spot. On my
count. . . Five, four, three, two, one. . . .

SUDDENLY the lights in the theatre go out and a single spotlight hits Ray. Miraculously the crowd goes silent.

RAY
I've made up my mind. . .
To live in memory of the lonesome time. . .

RAELETTES
I can't stop wanting you. . .

RAY
It's useless to say. . .
So I'll just live my life in dreams
of yesterday. . .

INT. CLEVELAND THEATRE–STAGE–NIGHT–1962
Jeff supervises the loading of the equipment.

JEFF
Okay, Guys, you got ten minutes to load up. Change
at the hotel.

MILT SHAW
They bought that country jive, hook, line and sinker.
You're amazing.

RAY
It ain't that. Country always tells a story. . .

MILT SHAW *(Joe signals Milt)*
Ray, I'd like you to meet Joe Adams. . . Hal Ziegler
hired Joe as the announcer for the rest of the tour.

RAY *(shaking Joe's hand)*
The Mayor of Melody. . . I recognized your voice. . .
used to listen to your radio show in L.A. in the 50s.

LANDMARK MOMENTS

As I mentioned earlier, Ray Charles revolutionized American music when he combined gospel and blues music in the early 1950s. Then, in 1962, he did it again.

Up to that time, country music was basically white people's music but Ray had grown up in the South listening to the Grand Ole Opry every week. He loved those country songs and had even played in an integrated country band, The Florida Playboys, in the late 1940s.

By 1962 Ray was established as one of the most successful R&B singers in the country. In the public's mind, his style was indelible, but Ray decided to break the mold and record an all country-and-western album.

Ray's record company, ABC Paramount, was flabbergasted by this decision and predicted that singing country music would kill Ray's career. But Ray Charles always believed that if he sincerely felt the music, he could sing anything. So he recorded *Modern Sounds in Country and Western Music* which became the best-selling album of 1962, produced the best-selling single of the year, "I Can't Stop Loving You," and won for Ray the honor of Recording Artist of the Year. Today, musicians like Willie Nelson and George Jones still consider *Modern Sounds in Country and Western Music* to be one of the greatest country-and-western records ever recorded.

—Taylor Hackford

JOE ADAMS
We've both come a ways since then.

RAY
What was all that countin' you was doin'
back there. . .

JOE ADAMS
Yes, I was cueing the lights down. . . it shuts up
the audience so you can sing a ballad instead of
having to scream it.

RAY
I'll be damned. . . who told you to do that?

JOE ADAMS
Nobody. . . it needed to be done.

RAY
Y'know how good it is for somebody to do what needs to
be done. . . 'stead of sayin', "That ain't my job?"

RAY *(cont'd)*
Come on, Joe, tell me 'bout Central Avenue. You ever
meet Jack Lauderdale?

JOE ADAMS
Hell yes. . . Jack and I used to chase tail together.

RAY
Yeah, he stole tail from me. . . .

Jeff's heard it all.

Ray's flashy big band arrangement of "Bye Bye Love" kicks
in and plays under a montage of Ray's success and Joe's rise.

EXT. SAENGER THEATRE MARQUEE–CHICAGO–NIGHT–1962

JOE ADAMS (V.O.)
Hello, Chicago. . .

INT. THE CHICAGO STAGE–NIGHT–1962
Ray and the Raelettes are on stage, singing "Bye-Bye Love."

EXT. ANOTHER THEATRE–DAY–1962
Jeff drags in a heavy trunk as Ray and Joe stand, smoking.

FATHEAD
Jeff, hurry up, man, we gotta rehearse.

RAY
Hey, Jeff, did you know that Joe starred in the movie
Carmen Jones for. . . who was that director?

JOE ADAMS
Otto Preminger.

RAY
. . . and he starred on Broadway with Lena Horne.

JOE ADAMS
She was the star. . . I was supporting.

JEFF *(yanking open the trunk)*
That a fact. . . ?

JOE ADAMS
Got a surprise for you, Ray. . . . *(taking out a magazine)*
You've got the cover of *Cash Box*: "The Nation's Hottest
Selling Album—*Modern Sounds of Country & Western*."

Ray laughs as Joe shakes his hand. Jeff just watches them. . .

JOE (cont'd) (brandishing the article)
Ray, you're hotter than hell. All your concerts are
selling out and your record sales are bigger than
ever. You're entering a whole new tax bracket.
You've gotta start looking for shelters. Why let
Uncle Sam take it all? Real estate is a winner.

RAY
I don't understand about this stuff, but I'm willing
to learn.

JOE ADAMS
I've been investing in real estate in LA for the past 12
years and it hasn't been bad.

Ray leans in, listening intently to Joe.

INT. VARIOUS THEATERS–NIGHT–1963
A series of quick cuts: Joe announces Ray's show in various
theaters as the music continues. . . .

JOE
Hello, New York. . . Hello, St. Louis. . . Hello, Miami!

A BILLBOARD "TOP 100" CHART–1963
is suddenly ANIMATED. Ray's album rises like the mercury
on a summer day. . . soaring from #55, all the way to #1.

INT. SAM CLARK'S ABC OFFICES–DAY–1963–
MUSIC CONTINUES
SAM CLARK (into phone)
Ray, I've finally got religion! Billboard just said
you're the number one artist of 1962, "Can't Stop
Loving You" is the top single. . . and "Modern
Sounds" is album of the year! We've sold three
million units. . . it doesn't get any better than this!

INT. RAY AND DELLA'S HEPBURN STREET HOME–BEDROOM–
DAY–1963
INTERCUT: Ray—alone in his and Della's bedroom—cooking
a spoon of heroin, with a phone cradled to his ear. He inter-
jects the above conversation, then—

RAY (into phone)
Let's hope it gets better than that, 'cause that
record is really hot, man. An' tomorrow, we
leave for Europe. . . that should goose up sales
over there. Another million, 'cause those bobby-
soxers really dig it and Quincy already laid the track.

DELLA
Ray, Jeff's downstairs. You finished packin'?

RAY
I'm coming. . .

DELLA
Ray come on now.

RAY
I heard you the first time I said it.

RAY (cont'd)
I gotta go now. Talk to you later.

He hangs up, lays down the spoon. Takes out a syringe. . .

DELLA
That's fine Ray, I'll meet you downstairs.

INT. RAY AND DELLA'S HEPBURN STREET HOME–HALLWAY–
DAY–1963
She knows what's happening. She turns and leaves.

FADE TO BLACK:

EXT. ORLY AIRPORT–DAY–1963 (STOCK)
A DC-7 airplane roaring as it lands, all four propellers shred-
ding the mist.

JOE ADAMS (V.O.)
L'homme que le monde entier attendait! Mesdames,
Mesdemoiselles, Messieurs—Monsieur Ray Charles!

The SOUND of thunderous applause as the music resumes. . .

EXT. L'ETOILE–PARIS (STOCK SHOT)–DAY–1963

STAGE OUTFITS

After completing my research for the film, I decided I wanted an even more vibrant look for the Raelettes. So I took the basic silhouettes from the time periods and enhanced the colors, especially for the Raelettes' wardrobe. Their performance clothes were more vibrant than their street clothes. They were not supposed to be sex kittens but I brought the necklines down and made the dresses more form fitting so they were a little sexy. We used oranges, reds, and blues to kick it up a bit. When Ray wore a red tuxedo, the girls would wear red dresses because that was how they dressed in the late fifties and early sixties.

—Sharen Davis, costume designer

ABOVE: Some of the many costume drawings by Sharen Davis.

EXT. STAGE DOOR–OLYMPIA THEATRE, PARIS (STOCK)–NIGHT–1963

Ray and Joe walk out the stage door. . . and they're swarmed by fans. JOE'S VOICE ECHOES in the background, shouting over the cheers of distant crowds:

> **JOE ADAMS** (V.O.)
> Pronto, Roma. . . ! Guten Abend, Frankfurt. . . ! Buenas Noches, Madrid. . . ! Oregato, Tokyo. . . !

EXT. NEW BALDWIN HILLS HOME–DAY–1964–MUSIC CONTINUES

Joe gets out of a Mercedes. . . followed by Ray and Della. . . carrying their new baby boy, ROBERT. Ray looks excited, but Della just peers up at the mansion. . .

EXT. NEW BALDWIN HILL'S HOME–DAY–1964–MUSIC CONTINUES

> **JOE ADAMS**
> Bea, there's a park at the end of the street for the boys. . . you can see the whole L.A. basin from there. . . not even Beverly Hills has views like this.

INT. NEW BALDWIN HILLS HOME–DAY–1964

They enter a two-story atrium, featuring a grand staircase.

> **JOE ADAMS**
> The foyer is designed to impress anybody who walks through. Ray, there's a big staircase just like *Gone with the Wind*.

> **RAY** (laughing)
> Bea, we should get our portraits painted like . . . Rhett and Scarlet.

> **JOE ADAMS** (pointing through door)
> Bea, bring him in here. . . Ray, wait till you see what's waiting for you in the living room. I had them build you a solid marble fireplace two stories high.

> **RAY** (jumping with excitement)
> Hot damn. . . What do ya think, Bea?

> **DELLA** (cool, distant)
> It's awful big.

> **JOE ADAMS** (proudly)
> 8,500 square feet. . .

> **RAY**
> Biggest house in the neighborhood.

> **JOE ADAMS**
> Come on, Ray, let me show you your private office.

Joe leads Ray off. Ray calls for Jeff to follow. Della stands there alone looking lost.

EXT. BATON ROUGE AIRPORT–DAY–1964

Ray and the band disembark from the twin engine plane. A dozen Louisiana State Troopers greet Ray, Joe, and Jeff. A young officer steps forward.

> **A STATE TROOPER**
> Mr. Charles? I'm Sergeant Hale, Louisiana State Police. . . we're here to escort you to the State Capitol.

INT. BATON ROUGE AIRPORT–DAY–1964

Screaming fans greet Ray, Joe, Jeff, and Fathead as they walk through the arrival gate, into the terminal. The State Troopers fight to keep them back.

> **JOE** (holding up pieces of paper)
> These are personally signed by Ray Charles and you'll each get one if you take one step back.

Ray is anxious, fidgety. . . hungry for a fix.

> **RAY** (shaking his hand)
> Can we go to the hotel first. . . ?

> **STATE TROOPER**
> I'm sorry. . . but there's no time. The Governor's scheduled your ceremony for three o'clock sharp. Please follow me.

No time for a fix. Ray is getting desperate.

RAY *(to Joe)*
I'm not going to take the band to Baton Rouge.
Go ahead and get them on the bus.

JOE
Are you sure, Ray?

RAY
Positive.

Joe walks away after the State Troopers and fans. Ray turns to Fathead.

RAY *(cont'd)*
Fathead, get my coat. . . let's hit the can.

Fathead leads him into the restroom. Joe steps up to the Troopers.

JOE
Sergeant. . . I'd like to inspect the limo
Mr. Charles is riding in.

As the Sergeant leads Joe away, Jeff hurries the band members along, gazing anxiously in the direction that Ray and Fathead have gone.

INT. BATON ROUGE AIRPORT–RESTROOM–DAY– 1964– CONTINUOUS
Jeff walks up to the door of the men's room. He opens it and peers in.

JEFF
Ray, you in there? (where y'all at?)

Jeff's eyes widen: Fathead is cooking a spoonful while Ray ties himself off.

RAY
What y'all want? We ain't ready yet.

JEFF
What're you doin' Ray? You tryin' to
get arrested?

Jeff closes the door and looks around, Troopers everywhere and one of the biggest plods toward him.

JEFF *(cont'd)*
Ray, goddammit, you gotta come out of there.

RAY (O.S.)
Goddammit, I said we ain't ready yet.

INT. BATON ROUGE AIRPORT–DAY–1964–CONTINUOUS
Jeff feels a tap on his shoulder. A big Trooper stands waiting.

JEFF
How you doin' officer. Already two in there. . . an' I'm next.

BIG TROOPER
Hurry 'em up. . . I'm gonna piss my pants.

The big Trooper stands next to Jeff, waiting in line. Jeff is about to piss his pants. . .

JEFF
You guys gotta come outta there. I gotta go to the bathroom real bad. *(to the Trooper)* I don't know what's taking them so long, officer.

RAY *(stoned out of his mind)*
Hey, baby. . . the Gov ain't gonna bust his
favorite son.

EXT. LOUISIANA STATE CAPITOL–DAY–1964
CLOSE-UP: Governor JIMMY DAVIS, songwriter, politician,
scoundrel.

GOVERNOR JIMMIE DAVIS
On behalf of the great state of Louisiana. . .
and, of course, me personally, since I wrote
her great anthem. . .

EXT. LOUISIANA STATE CAPITOL–DAY–1964
A stoned Ray, surrounded by legislators.

GOVERNOR JIMMIE DAVIS
. . . I present to you, Mr. Ray Charles, this
proclamation. . . making you a "Favorite Son"
of Louisiana!

Everyone applauds as Davis begins to sing "You Are My
Sunshine."

FATHEAD & JEFF

FATHEAD
Man, that is so hip. . . now that's what I
call a politician.

JEFF *(nervous)*
Be cool, man, there are police all over
this place.

SEGUE to Ray's brilliant, big band arrangement of the song.

EXT. RPM HEADQUARTERS, L.A.–DAY–1964–
MUSIC CONTINUES
Ray's new headquarters, two stories, simple but impressive. . .

INT. RPM HEADQUARTERS, L.A.–DAY–1964–
MUSIC CONTINUES
Joe leads Ray through the new lobby, followed by Jeff.

He knocks again.

JEFF *(cont'd)*
C'mon outta there, guys.

Fathead and Ray finally drift out of the restroom. Jeff takes a
deep breath, hustling them off. . .

JEFF *(cont'd) (to the Trooper)*
Everything's cool. You can go ahead.

As they walk away.

JEFF *(cont'd)*
Boss. . . you got a death wish?

JOE
To the left is the secretary's office and your office
is to the right.

Joe leads Ray and Jeff into a huge office. . .

JOE *(cont'd)*
I want to report that it is twice the size of
Hepburn Street. There's a bathroom to your
left and my adjoining office behind you.
There's a full bar to your left. . . and a bottle
of Bols in the middle. On the wall we've got
your trophies and awards.

Jeff peers into Joe's office: It's as grand as Ray's.

INT. RPM HEADQUARTERS–RECORDING STUDIO–DAY–1964
Joe leads Ray and Jeff into a plush recording studio.

JOE
Here it is Ray. Your new recording studio.

ABOVE: The real RPM studio was used in the film.

On September 6, 1963, "Ray C. Robinson and
Della B. Robinson, husband and wife as joint
tenants," bought from Ernest and Cora Warren, for
$52,000, 2107 West Washington Boulevard, two lots
a few blocks east of Western Avenue and just north of
the Santa Monica Freeway. The lots looked as anonymous as any hundred feet along a Los Angeles
boulevard can look: an out-of-business gas station
and a small house set in a shabby but respectable
Negro neighborhood. Yet if any of Ray Charles'
actions deserve a drumroll and a trumpet fanfare,
buying 2107 West Washington Boulevard stands
among them. This anonymous three-eighths of an
acre became in time Ray's true home on earth. The
building he built there, its offices, recording studio,
and bachelor pad, became his castle, his fortress, his
faraway island; the place where he could work and
play and live and love and be by himself whenever
he pleased. For the next thirty years and more, no
matter how often or how far he wandered, Ray always
came home to 2107 West Washington Boulevard.
With one night off between gigs on the East Coast,
he'd fly home to 2107 just, as a longtime associate
put it, "to touch the walls."
—Michael Lydon, *Ray Charles*, 1998

RAY
With everything I asked for?

JOE
Totally "state-of-the art." Tom Dowd built the eight-track mixing console, you got two recorders, the works.

RAY *(laughing, delighted)*
No more payin' for studio time.

JOE
From now on, *we'll* be chargin' ABC. . .

JEFF
An' where's my office?

JOE
Right here, Jeff. We knew you'd want to be near the band.

Jeff goes to the door Joe's indicated, opens it. . . and his face drops. He's staring into a cubby-hole.

Joe and Ray walk away.

INT. NEW BALDWIN HILLS HOME–FOYER–DAY–1964
Two painted portraits of Ray and Della (Ray in red tux and Della in ball gown) adorn the wall at the top of the stairs.

Suddenly three little boys in baseball uniforms run down the stairs and out onto the patio.

EXT. NEW BALDWIN HILLS HOME–DAY–1964
Ray listens to Della's play-by-play commentary on Ray Jr.'s exploits in the swimming pool. David frolics in the shallow end, while Jeff cooks hot dogs and hamburgers on the BBQ.

DELLA
C'mon Ray. He's jumping on the board, he's walking to the edge. . . there he goes. . . cannonball! But he's not holding his knees. . .

Ray laughs as he HEARS the splash. The telephone rings. The housekeeper, who is holding young Robert, answers it. Della turns to Ray.

DELLA *(cont'd)*
Go get the phone, baby. . .

Ray walks over to the bar and takes the receiver.

RAY *(into phone)*
Hello. . . sure, I remember who you are. *(listening)* Dear God. . . no. When?. . . How did it happen?. . .

Ray steadies himself. . . stricken.

RAY *(cont'd)*
Yes. . . I'll catch a plane. I'll be there as soon as possible. . . Oh God. . .

DELLA
Ray. . . what happened?

RAY *(hangs up)*
Margie. . . she's dead.

DELLA
Oh, my God. . . how?

RAY
She. . . overdosed. . .

That hits Della. Ray can feel her stare. . .

RAY (cont'd) (subdued)
I didn't start her, Bea. She never did dope while
she was with me. . . I wouldn't let her.

DELLA
Yeah, Ray. . . I'm sure you set a fine example.

He can't bear her ridicule, not now. He turns away, retreating
to the house. . . until Della's words stop him:

DELLA (cont'd)
What about her baby. . . ?

Ray is stunned. . .

RAY
You knew?

DELLA
His name's Charles Wayne.

RAY (beat)
Baby's fine. He's with her sister. . .

DELLA
I'll start sendin' 'im money.

RAY
It's already done, Bea. . . ev'ry month.

For an instant, all is laid bare in this long, complicated mar-
riage. . . and it's more than Ray can take. He stops and cries.
Ashamed, he retreats into the house. Della takes a step to follow him, to comfort him. . . but she can't. She turns to watch
her own children, playing in the sun.

FADE TO BLACK:

INT. RPM RECORDING STUDIO–DAY–1964–MUSIC CONTINUES
Joe stands at the door, checking musicians off a list as they enter the room. Jeff is handing out music.

JOE
In five minutes Mr. Charles will be here and he will be ready to go. The charts that Jeff is handing out should be returned at the end of rehearsal.

Fathead rushes in.

JOE (cont'd)
You're late. . . that's a fifty-dollar fine.

FATHEAD
I ain't late!

JEFF
I give 'em a ten-minute grace period, Joe.

JOE
Five after two—he's late. We are docking his pay fifty dollars.

FATHEAD
WHAT!!! Where's Ray?!

JOE
You don't have to talk to Ray—you're talking to me.

FATHEAD
I'll talk to whoever I damn well please! An' it sure as hell ain't you!

Fathead stalks off.

**INT. RAY'S RPM OFFICE–DAY–MOMENTS LATER–1964–
MUSIC CONTINUES**
Ray turns as Fathead storms in, Joe and Jeff close behind.

FATHEAD
Ray, this fool Joe Adams is tryin' to fine me for bein' late!

RAY
What time you get here?

FATHEAD (shocked)
What? Jes' now! The band is still settin' up, man! Jeff never. . . .

JOE ADAMS (interrupting)
I'm not Jeff.

FATHEAD
That's a fact, Jack!

JEFF
Ray, you said, the band's my thing?

RAY
It is.

JEFF (glaring at Joe)
Then Fathead, go back to rehearsal.

FATHEAD (conciliatory)
Ray, you know how it is, man. You've been there. . .

Ray sits there stone-faced, inscrutable.

JEFF
Go on, Fathead, let me handle this.

Fathead leaves.

JEFF (cont'd)
You wanna tell me,what the hell's goin' on?

JOE ADAMS (answering for Ray)
I'm not doing anything I haven't been asked to do. Ray's running a business, and he shouldn't have to waste time hearing someone is late.

JEFF
I'm not talking to you Joe. I'm talking to Ray. (to Ray) Ray, listen, when I was in combat, I had to lead men into places they didn't wanna go, but they went. . . and some of 'em didn't come back. They went 'cause I asked

'em to. . . I know you think I'm soft on the band, but those cats'll do whatever I ask. . . *(to Joe)* . . . but if you come in here with this "running a business" crap, you're gonna lose some good people, I'm telling you.

JOE ADAMS
There's musicians waiting in line to play for Ray Charles.

JEFF
Not for long, once they get a taste of you. *(turns to Ray)* Ray, you're the leader. . . be one!

RAY
Jeff, things have changed, this ain't the days when the seven of us worked the chitlin' circuit. . . an' if you weren't so busy, buildin' that bowlin' alley, maybe you would see that.

JEFF *(looking at Joe Adams)*
So, you know 'bout that, huh?

RAY
I know everything. . . the question is, how did you do it?

JEFF
You think I'm stealin', Ray?

RAY
If the Shaw Agency is gonna give you a cut of the

10 percent I'm givin' 'em, they might as well leave the money in my pocket.

JEFF *(to Joe Adams)*
Why don't you leave us alone?

JOE ADAMS
Ray?

RAY
Step outside, Joe.

JOE ADAMS
I'll be in my office.

Joe goes out and Jeff turns to Ray.

JEFF
I don't know why (that) jealous bastard planted that lie, but I never stole from you an' I never will. . . I got a small business loan an' yes, Milt Shaw was payin' me a little extra—but I'm no thief, Ray.

Ray lays an envelope on his desk.

RAY
What 'bout this Jeff? A promoter swearin' you made side deals with 'im to split my overages. . .

Jeff has no answer.

RAY *(cont'd)*
How could you do that, man? We were like brothers.

JEFF
If we were like brothers, why'd you pay Joe more than me?! I've been takin' care of you, since Lowell Fulson!

RAY
You broke my heart, man.

JEFF
You know what? You broke mine a long time ago.

RAY
There it is.

JEFF
You know what? You're gonna get yours someday and I pray to God he has mercy on your soul, you son of a bitch!

Jeff storms out. Joe comes back in.

JOE
You alright, Ray?

CUT TO:

EXT. NEW BALDWIN HILLS HOME–DAY–1964
Ray Jr. is brimming with excitement as Joe opens the car door for Ray. Della hovers over her son, delighted for him.

RAY JR.
Hey, Dad. . . I made the All-Star team! The game's on Thursday!

RAY
That's great. . . dammit. I'm not gonna be here, I'll be on tour. . . how 'bout I buy the team some new uniforms? You tell the coach, no matter how much it costs.

Ray Jr. is devastated, but he does what kids do for part-time dads—he smiles.

RAY JR.
Okay. . .

JOE
Hey son, do you want to take your dad's briefcase?

Ray Jr. gets the briefcase and runs into the house.

JOE *(cont'd) (to Ray)*
The plane to Montreal leaves at 11. I'll pick you up at 8:30.

RAY
Okay.

Della takes Ray's arm, and leads him toward the house.

DELLA *(quietly)*
Did you what hear Ray Jr. said to you?

RAY
Yeah. . .

DELLA
Do you know how much makin' the All-Stars means to him?

RAY *(beat)*
Bea. . . I had to fire Jeff today.

DELLA
What?!

RAY
He was stealin' from me. . .

DELLA
Jeff? I don't believe it!

RAY
It's true. . . *(subdued)* We're better off without 'im.

Joe starts up the car. Della turns at the sound. Joe nods a greeting to her, but she ignores him and goes into the house after Ray.

FADE TO BLACK:

INT. MONTREAL THEATRE–NIGHT–1964

JOE (V.O.)
Bon soir, Montréal. . .

Despite everything, Ray is still rocking the house. The band and the Raelettes are at their prime. . .

Ray begins to sing "Hard Times."

EXT. LOGAN AIRPORT–BOSTON–DAY–1964–
MUSIC CONTINUES
A light snow is on the ground as Ray's plane taxies to the hangar, rolling to a stop. The band begins to exit from the airplane. Joe appears, helping Ray down the steps.

    A MAN'S VOICE
    Excuse me gentlemen—U.S. Customs!

Joe glances up: Two CUSTOMS AGENTS step out of the shadows, flashing their badges.

    CUSTOMS AGENT #1
    We're going to need some identification. . .

Everyone fishes out their passports.

    CUSTOMS AGENT #2
    You just arrived from Montreal?

    JOE
    Yes, is there a problem?

    CUSTOMS AGENT #2
    We were alerted there might be drugs on this plane.

    JOE
    What. . . ? That's outrageous! I want to call
    our lawyer. . .

    CUSTOMS AGENT #2
    No lawyers at international checkpoints. Now,
    we're going to have to search everyone on this
    plane. Mr. Charles, if you don't mind, we'll start
    with you. I'd like to see your overcoat.

    RAY *(an edge)*
    If I don't mind. . . ?

    JOE
    Don't say anything, Ray.

Ray lets them take it. He's an old pro at this by now. . . not at

all hysterical. The agent reaches into the vest pocket. CLOSER ON Ray's face. . . his cool demeanor beginning to melt.

    CUSTOMS AGENT#2 *(finding container)*
    What's this?

    RAY
    Medicine for my stomach.

    CUSTOMS AGENT#2 *(not buying it)*
    You'll have to stay here at the airport until we've
    had a chance to analyze this.

Ray's face is stoic, but he knows he's screwed.

    JOE
    If you're going to search us, we insist on having our
    attorneys present. . .

INT. SAM CLARK'S ABC OFFICES–DAY–MUSIC CONTINUES–
1965
Sam Clark looks across the desk at Ray and Joe.

    SAM CLARK
    Ray, this is not some judge in Indiana, it's federal. . .
    they can charge you with smuggling which is real
    prison time. Our lawyers will do what we can, but. . .

It's beginning to sink in. Ray's in big trouble.

                          FADE TO BLACK:

INT. NEW BALDWIN HILLS HOME–RAY'S OFFICE–DAY–1965
A ringing telephone shatters the silence. Della's hand lifts the receiver. . .

    DELLA
    Hello. . .

Ray's fingers cover hers, forcing it back.

Ray slouches on a chair. Della stands over him.

    DELLA *(cont'd)*
    You can't hide out here forever, Ray.

RAY
This is my house, Bea. . . I ain't in prison yet.

DELLA
No, this is my house! You ain't been here more 'n six days since we moved in!

Ray rises, heads toward the bathroom. . . but Della blocks him.

RAY
What you doin'? Get out my way. . .

DELLA
No, Ray. . . A needle ain't gonna solve this. . .

He has no answer to that. He's lost. . .

DELLA *(cont'd) (gentler now)*
Ray. . . don't you know by now? Nothin' on earth can help you. God's the only one. . .

RAY
God. . . ? *(a quiet intensity)* You got any idea what it's like to go blind. . . and you're still afraid of the dark? To pray to God to leave ya. . . jes' a lil' bit of light? *(bitterly)* God don't listen to people like me.

DELLA
Stop talkin' like that!

RAY
Why should I?! Me an' God are even, so I can do whatever I damn well please! An' if I wanna shoot dope, I'm gonna shoot dope, so get outta my way!

Della measures him a moment. Then. . .

DELLA
Go ahead then. *(she steps aside)* But you walk through that door, I'm gonna do what I shoulda done a long time ago. . . take my boys an' leave.

RAY *(darkly)*
You ain't takin' my boys. . . an' you ain't leavin' neither 'cause you got no place to go.

DELLA
No place. . . ? *(a bitter laugh)* You think I'm scared of losin' this?

She opens her arms, indicating the house, their possessions.

DELLA *(cont'd)*
The only thing I was ever scared of losin' was you. Where was I gonna find another Ray Robinson?

Despite himself, that touches Ray.

DELLA *(cont'd)*
So I put up with some terrible stuff. . . an' I guess that makes me part to blame. Only. . . I ain't scared no more.

Della turns and starts to walk away.

RAY
Bea. . . wait. *(she stops)* I love you an' 'em boys. . . more 'n anything else in the world.

DELLA
That's a damn lie, and you know it! *(taking a trophy off the mantle)* Ever take a look at this. . . ? Really look at it. Ray Charles Jr.'s "Most Valuable Player." He was so proud that day. . . till you came home, too loaded to go to his banquet. *(beat)* There's only one thing you love. . . more than me an' the boys, more than all those women you slept with on the road. . . even more than all your dope you ever took.

RAY
What're you talkin' 'bout. . . ?

DELLA
Your music. But if you keep usin' that needle, they're gonna take your music away. . . an' lock you up.

For the first time. . . Ray is terrified.

DELLA *(cont'd)*
Is that poison worth losin' everything. . . ?

For once, Ray is speechless. Della walks out. He listens to her footsteps. . . to the sound of the door, closing. Ray runs his fingers over the trophy. . . then drops his head and cries.

FADE TO BLACK:

INT. BLACKNESS–NIGHT–1965
We HEAR Ray hyperventilating, crying out in pain.

INT. ST. FRANCIS CLINIC–RAY'S ROOM–DAY/NIGHT–1965
Ray appears in a hospital room. . . awakening alone in a fathomless space, sweating profusely—the torture of withdrawal. He falls out of bed, nurses help him back. He rushes to the bathroom, vomiting. . .

A doctor appears, Dr. Frederick Hacker.

DR. HACKER
Mr. Charles, you don't have to go through this. We have a substitute that can help wean you off heroin.

RAY *(in agony)*
No, Doc. . . I gotta do this on my own.

Dr. Hacker shakes his head. . . he knows what's to come. He gently removes Ray's glasses.

DR. HACKER
Okay, we'll do it your way.

NIGHT CHANGES TO DAY

Ray's tortuous journey continues. The bed is drenched in sweat. He soils himself. He thrashes continuously.

Another day passes.

INT. ST. FRANCIS HOSPITAL–RAY'S ROOM–NIGHT–1965
Ray is alone in the void again, seemingly floating in darkness. Suddenly, Ray throws back the blankets and rushes into the bathroom, puking his guts out. In a moment a nurse appears and rushes to help him. Dr. Hacker appears as they place him gently back on the bed.

DR. HACKER
He's got no liquids left. . . get an IV in him right away.

On the bed Ray writhes in agony.

DISSOLVE TO:

TIGHT ON RAY'S ARM
Ray is lying on the bed as the nurses prep him for an IV.

NURSE
Mr. Charles, we're going to give you an IV to get fluids into you. The tourniquet will be a little tight. Alcohol please. Now, I'm going to insert the needle. . .

Ray hears those words and reacts.

RAY
No. . . no needles.

He bolts for the door. The nurses follow.

NURSE
We've got a runner.

Two burly ORDERLIES grab Ray and throw him back on the bed as restraints are slapped on him. Dr. Hacker appears in the doorway.

DOCTOR HACKER
Easy, easy. Restrain him gently.

INT. ST. FRANCIS HOSPITAL–COMMUNITY ROOM–DAY
Ray and Dr. Hacker sit together playing chess. Ray's scratching himself uncontrollably, possessed by physical and mental cravings. Dr. Hacker makes his move, checkmate.

RAY
Damn, you whipped my ass again, but I'm learnin'. . . you ain't gonna beat me the same way twice.

LANDMARK MOMENTS

In the movie, we don't shrink away from Ray's drug use because you can't tell the story of Ray Charles without including this chapter of his life.

Ray described to me how incredibly lonely he was when he first started touring as a teenager. Often the other band members would exclude him from social activities because of his blindness. At that time (1940s), many great jazz musicians were famous for "getting high" and one of those social activities that Ray had been excluded from was drugs. He first started smoking pot when he was a teenager and later graduated to shooting heroin. However, Ray didn't exhibit the sloppiness that often characterizes addicts. In fact, he was probably the most functioning heroin addict on the planet. He never missed a gig; he was always on time; he had his band rehearsed; and he would record most of his songs in one take.

Ray shot heroine for twenty years, but he never encouraged others to join him. As he said, "It was my thing."

Of course, sooner or later, for anyone, addiction catches up with you. Ray was busted several times but managed to negotiate himself out of trouble. However, in 1964, at Boston's Logan Airport, U.S. customs officials discovered drugs on Ray when he arrived from Canada.

This bust was different, it was a federal rap and the penalties were potentially career ending. Now Ray had to make a choice: Give up heroine or give up his music. For Ray, it was obvious, he had to quit. He went to a rehab clinic in Los Angeles, and kicked heroine, *cold turkey.* For the next forty years, Ray never touched heroin again. This is true character. We did not try to preach in the film but this chapter of Ray's life delivers a very compelling lesson.

—Taylor Hackford

DR. HACKER
I spoke with the judge in Boston, and he'll agree to probation. . . *(off Ray's hopeful look) If* you finish my program and agree to take periodic drug tests.

RAY
I'll do it. . . I know no one believes me, but I'm finished with dope.

Dr. Hacker hesitates a moment.

DR. HACKER
Who's George. . . ?

This stops Ray cold. He turns away, silent.

DR. HACKER *(cont'd)*
Ray, you've come through the worst of the physical reactions, but now the mental cravings take over. . . and that's where you win or lose. We should begin psychotherapy sessions. . .

RAY *(stony)*
Forget the head-shrinking, Doc, I can handle this.

DR. HACKER
Mr. Charles, you're not the first celebrity junkie I've treated. Nobody cons me, at any price. If you want me to give that judge a positive report, you have to earn it.

Ray doesn't reply, feeling the chess pieces. . . stonewalling. Dr. Hacker sighs and walks out of the room.

RAY
Dr. Hacker. . . Dr. Hacker. . .

No answer. He scratches his body, uneasy. The doctor's ultimatum has pissed him off.

What's worse, he still wants a fix. . . He misjudges the space and walks into a table. Suddenly, he explodes, smashing his fist down onto the table. Ray turns away angrily, trips. . . and falls. He starts to pull himself to his feet when he senses something. . . water on the floor. He reaches out. . . and his hand touches cold metal—Aretha's old galvanized rinse tub.

He lunges his hands into the tub's murky water, thrashes around, groping for George.

ARETHA (V.O.)
He ain't in there.

EXT. ROBINSON HOME–DAY–1935
Ray jumps back in shock. He's back in Jellyroll and he can see the old bottle tree. Aretha sits in her rocking chair on the front porch.

ARETHA
Talk to me, son, I ain't no bad dream, I'm part of you. Still your mama. Even all that dope couldn't keep me away.

Ray walks over to the porch.

RAY
Mama, I kept my promise.

ARETHA
Y'heard my words, not my meanin'. You got strong alright. . . went places I never dreamed of, but ya still became a cripple. *(he looks down, ashamed)* Come'ere, baby.

He sits on the porch next to her rocking chair and lays his head in her lap. Ray hugs her legs, feeling her strength. Then he opens his eyes and sees the four-year-old George walk out the front door.

> Ain't nobody gonna ask me when it's time for me to go. So I figure, it ain't my decision. When it comes to that, whatever is gonna be is gonna be. While you're here, you just try to shift the odds in your favor as much as you can. But that's all you can do.
>
> —Ray Charles, Michael Lydon, *Ray Charles*, 1998

GEORGE (gently)
Ray. . . You gotta stop livin' for the both of us. . .
it wasn't your fault. . .

Ray takes George in his arms, holding him like he'll never let him go. His mother looks down on her two sons.

ARETHA
Now promise us, you'll never let nobody or nothin' turn you into no cripple ever again. . . that you'll always stand on your own two feet. . .

Ray hears the true meaning of those childhood words, looks up at his mother and smiles.

RAY
I promise.

FADE TO BLACK

FADE UP ON A MONTAGE OF RAY'S ALBUM COVERS FROM 1965–2001.

SUPER OVER MONTAGE OF RAY'S ALBUM COVERS:

Over the next 40 years Ray continued to make
hit records, win Grammys and sell out concerts,
becoming one of the world's most beloved entertainers.

SUPER OVER EXT. GEORGIA STATE CAPITOL:

And yet, his proudest moment came in 1979
at the Georgia State Capitol

CUT TO: INT. GEORGIA STATE HOUSE - DAY - 1979

JULIAN BOND
Today, we're here to right a wrong that was done to one of our native sons nearly twenty years ago.

JULIAN BOND speaks to a full chamber of the legislature. Ray stands tall behind him with Della and their three grown sons.

JULIAN BOND (cont'd)
In 1961, Ray Charles was banned from performing in the state of Georgia because he refused to play

184

before a segregated audience. Thankfully, we've come a long way since then. Some of us have fought for equality through the political process. . . but Ray Charles changed American culture by touching peoples' hearts. So on this day—March 7, 1979—we, the duly elected representatives of the State of Georgia, not only proclaim "Georgia on My Mind" our official state song. . . we also offer Mr. Ray Charles a public apology and welcome him back home.

Everyone in the chamber rises, giving Ray a standing ovation.

DELLA (*whispering to Ray*)
If only your mama was here.

RAY
She's here. She ain't never left. . .

FADE TO BLACK:

CUT TO JELLYROLL and IMAGE OF ARETHA PICKING UP YOUNG RAY BEFORE HE LEAVES FOR THE STATE SCHOOL FOR THE BLIND. FREEZE ON THAT IMAGE:

SUPER OVER FREEZE FRAME OF ARETHA & YOUNG RAY:
Ray kept his promise. He never touched heroin again. As celebrated as he became, he never forgot his roots, contributing over $20 million to African-American colleges and charities for the blind and deaf.

Ray Charles Robinson
1930–2004

THE GENIUS OF RAY CHARLES

ATLANTIC 1312

VOLCANIC ACTION OF MY SOUL
RAY CHARLES

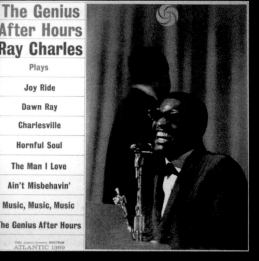

The Genius After Hours
Ray Charles

Plays

Joy Ride

Dawn Ray

Charlesville

Hornful Soul

The Man I Love

Ain't Misbehavin'

Music, Music, Music

The Genius After Hours

ATLANTIC 1369

RAY CHARLES
DOING HIS THING

RAY CHARLES AND
BETTY CARTER

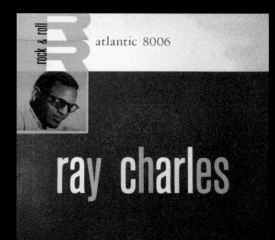

rock & roll

atlantic 8006

ray charles

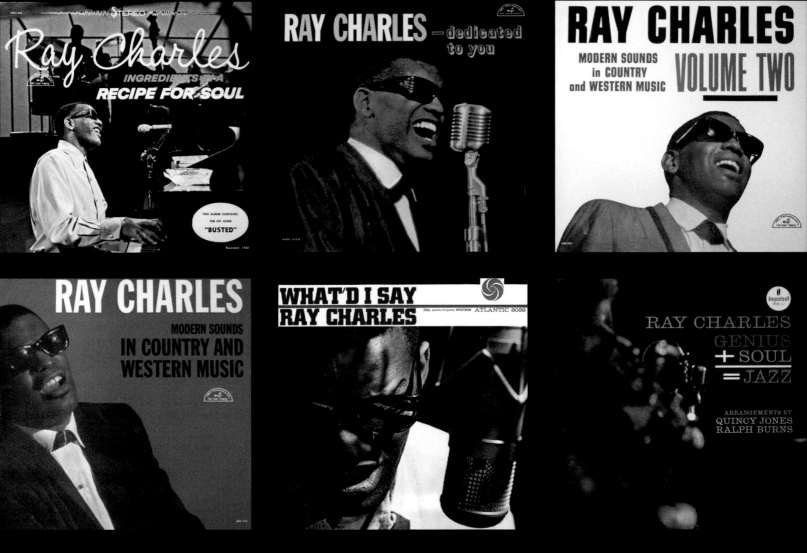

A Tribute to Ray Charles
September 10, 1930–June 10, 2004

LAST WORDS OF BROTHER RAY

by David Ritz

LEFT: Studio portrait of the always well-dressed Ray Charles, 1955, which was used for publicity purposes.

Why did Christopher Columbus discover America? To bring the world Ray Charles.

—Paul Schaffer,
Rolling Stone, July 8-22, 2004

Reprinted in a slightly revised version from *Rolling Stone* (July 8-22, 2004), used by permission of the author. David Ritz has collaborated with, among others, Marvin Gaye, Aretha Franklin, B.B. King, Smokey Robinson, and the Neville brothers, on their life stories.

"Death," Ray Charles told me when he first learned that cancer was devouring his body, "is the one thing that ain't ever going away."

I met Ray Charles in 1975, when he agreed to let me ghostwrite his autobiography. He was vulgar, refined, funny, sexy, spontaneous, outlandish, brave, brutal, tender, blue, ecstatic. He would wrap his arms around his torso, hugging himself in a grand gesture of self-affirmation. In normal conversation, he preached and howled and fell to the floor laughing. He was, in his own words, "raw-ass country."

Because my job was to take the material of our dialogues and weave them into a first-person narrative, I had to make sure the dialogues were deep. I began tentatively by saying, "Now if this question is too tough . . ."

"How can a question be too tough? The truth is the truth."

The truth—at least Ray's truth—came pouring out: that his life had been rough; that his life had been blessed; that he had followed his musical muse wherever it led; that he had been a junkie; that he had given up junk only when faced with prison; that every day he still drank lots of gin and smoked lots of pot and worked just as tirelessly; that he had a huge appetite for women; that he wasn't even certain how many children he had fathered; that he was unrepentant about it all.

"When my mother died, I didn't understand death," he told me. "Couldn't feature it. What do you mean, she's gone forever? I was fifteen, living at a school for the blind 160 miles away from home. She was all I had in the world. No, she couldn't be dead. Can't make it without her.

"That's when I saw what everyone sees: You can't make a deal with death. No, sir. And you can't make a deal with God. Death is cold blooded, and maybe God is, too. So I'm alone, and I'm going crazy, until a righteous Christian lady from the little country town where I grew up wakes me and shakes me and says, 'Boy, stop feeling sorry for yourself. You gotta' carry on.'"

I wondered if the experience made him more religious.

"Made me realize I had to depend on me," he shot back. "No one was going to do nothing for me. You hear me? No one. I could praise Jesus till I'm blue in the face. Pray till the cows come home. But Mama ain't coming back. So if Mama gave me religion, the religion said, 'Believe in yourself.'"

Early the next morning I was eager to continue the conversation. "Ray, I just wanted to ask you another question about death . . ."

"Look man," he said, irritated and tired, "I wouldn't talk to my mama now if she came out of the grave." And with that, he fell asleep.

Brother Ray: Ray Charles' Own Story came out in 1978. Ray liked the book because, as he said, "It's me—and I like me."

In the summer of 2003 he was having hip problems and was canceling his U.S. tour. Ray never cancels tours. I knew something was deeply wrong.

When I called Ray, he didn't sound like himself. "My liver's not right," he said. "I'm not putting out no press release, but I heard them use the word cancer."

A month later, my phone rang shortly after midnight. "I'm thinking," he said, "that we need to add some stuff to the book. But right now I'm tired. I'll call you when I can."

Weeks passed before he called. "Someone said," he told me, "that if you picture yourself well, you get well. If you can conceive it, you can achieve it. I'm focusing on the future."

"I'm getting stronger," he said the next time he called. "I can feel it."

"Great. Heard you talked to Mable."

Mable John, the great rhythm-and-blues artist for Motown and Stax/Volt, is a former lead Raelette and one of Ray's closest confidantes. Now she is a minister.

"Man, I been talking to Mable for forty years. For forty years she's been trying to save my sorry ass."

"Any progress?"

"How about you?" he asked.

"I've been reading the Bible."

"I got my Braille copy. Always keep it with me."

"What's it telling you?"

"When we were writing my book, I remember telling you that I'm not really looking at Jesus, I'm looking at God. Well, I'm looking at it differently now."

"How so?"

"I think about stories. Songs are stories. And if you're going to write a good song, you're going to have to praise a woman. That's the key. And if you're writing a book about God, you're going to have to praise God. That's what Jesus did. Praised his Father. Taught us about praise. I used to think all that church praise, all that hooting and hollering, was overdone. Stop shouting. Be cool. Besides, if God is God, why does he need all this praise? Now I'm thinking it ain't God who needs the praise—it's us who need to do the praising. The praise makes us stronger. That's why I'm getting stronger."

"What's the source of the strength?"

"Used to think it was me. But now I see my strength has limits. I used to think that I'm in control of this whole operation—my music, my band, my life, my ladies. But soon as you start thinking that way, brother, run for cover. 'Cause someone's about to kick your ass."

"Is God kicking your ass?"

"God's teaching me to depend on something I can't see. I've always seen ahead of myself—how to buy a car or buy a building, how to start a publishing company or a record label, how to make more bread this year than last. They call that foresight, don't they? Well, I've been blessed with foresight. Thank you, Jesus. But now it ain't serving me. Now I need another kind of sight."

A part of me wanted to see him; a part of me did not. But when Ray called and said I could come by the studio, I dropped everything and ran.

He was seated behind the control board. He looked smaller, thinner, certainly diminished but far from defeated. I thought of the thousands of hours he had spent here recording his voice. That voice, once an instrument of unprecedented power, was reduced to a whisper.

He was thinking about other musicians, now gone.

"Did I mention Erroll Garner in my book?" he asked, referring to the great jazz pianist.

"Can't remember. I think so."

"I think I talked too much about my own playing. Too much about myself.

"Being too much in a hurry. Too impatient. Looking for everything to be perfect. Lost my head. Said some nasty crap to guys who didn't deserve it. You know me, man. I'm always messing with the drummers. If they don't get my time, I pitch a bitch. Treat them bad. I feel like I hurt people. I know I hurt people. Well, tell them I'm not a bad guy. Tell them I have feelings, too. Tell them I appreciate them. Tell them . . . just tell them Brother Ray loves them."

The last time I saw him, we didn't speak. He could hardly speak at all. His deterioration was dramatic. I hadn't been able to reach him for six or seven weeks. His people told me he was talking to no one. Minister Mable Johns said otherwise.

"I was there the other day," she told me. "He's still going to his building every day. He's still goes into his studio. He's maintaining his routine. Routine is Ray's life. He'll never give up his routine. So they set up a bed for him

where he used to work. He has all the nurses he needs. He says he has all he needs to get through. And I believe him."

"Is he peaceful?" I asked.

"He's determined. He can't be any other way. He's determined to come outside today for the ceremony."

The outdoor ceremony was to commemorate Ray's beloved professional home, 2107 West Washington Boulevard, in Los Angeles, as a historical landmark. Mable and I arrived early and sat in the front row. The speeches droned on. And then the door to his building opened.

Seated in a wheelchair, Ray appeared in a crisply pressed pinstripe suit. He was in obvious pain. Slowly, carefully, he was lifted from the chair and brought to the podium, where his longtime manager Joe Adams brought the microphone to Ray's mouth. The sound of

the singer's voice was slight, distorted, slurred, his words barely audible. He thanked the city and then paused. I felt him struggling for energy, for a single stream of breath. Finally the breath came:

"I'm weak," he said, "but I'm getting stronger."

The news came six weeks later. Ray was gone. My reaction was immediate: I had to hear him sing. I put on his live versions of "Drown in My Own Tears" and "Tell the Truth." Those are the songs that bonded his heart to mine as a boy. After a good, long cry, I called Mable.

"I know he's alright," she said. "I know he's found his strength."

ABOVE: Ray Charles, a lifelong cigarette smoker, photographed on January 1, 1966, in his office at the RPM studio in Los Angeles.

1960s

It was always a real thrill for me to sing "What'd I Say" and think of Ray, so you can imagine how I felt when,

in 1986, Ray sang a version of our song, "Sail on Sailor." He was so brilliant, and he sang it better than we did.

Maybe most of all what I remember him for is his sensitive singing on cuts like "I Can't Stop Loving You."

You can be sure that the whole world will never stop loving you, Ray.

—Brian Wilson, *Rolling Stone,* July 8-22, 2004

ABOVE: RC on the balcony of the Hotel Claridge, with the Arc de Triomphe over his shoulder, during his first trip to Paris in October 1961.

This may sound like sacrilege, but I think Ray Charles was more important than Elvis Presley. I don't know if Ray was

the architect of rock and roll, but he was certainly the first guy to do a lot of things. He was not a snob about style.

Who the hell ever put so many styles together and made it work? He was a true American original.

—Billy Joel, *Rolling Stone,* July 8-22, 2004

ABOVE: Ray Charles performs in the studio with his back-up singers, The Raelettes, sometime during the early 1960s.

1960s

Chess came to Ray as love at first sight. Ray loved chess because, as he explained years later, "there's no luck in it. With cards, no matter how well you play, you ain't gonna win unless the cards fall for you. But in chess, it's my brain against yours! We start with the same pieces in the same places, the only advantage, if you call it that, is that one player moves first. You've got to outwit, out-think, and out-maneuver the other person, and he's thinking to outwit you." Ray always kept a chessboard at hand, and in time he became a superb player. Had he not been blind, Ray, with his athletic figure and competitive drive, would surely have played basketball, tennis or golf. Yet Ray's affinity for chess went beyond love of a game. In chess he found the perfect metaphor for how he already saw the world. Attack and retreat, hide and dare, plan five moves ahead. Ray Charles had been playing chess long before he knew a pawn from a bishop.

—Michael Lydon, *Ray Charles*, 1998

ABOVE: RC in action during a performance in London on May 21, 1963. RIGHT: Once he discovered the joys of chess, RC was rarely without a chess board.

One thing I liked about Brother Ray is that he got his own plane. That motivated me, and I started renting them after that, and pretty soon I bought me a little jet. See, if you've got a plane, you're not wearing your legs out. Ray was always positive about what he was doing, and I admire him most for that. I tell you one thing: He could see a lot better than those with eyes.

—James Brown, *Rolling Stone,* July 8-22, 2004

LEFT: Ray Charles and his manager, Joe Adams, waiting to board a private jet in January of 1966. ABOVE: RC, his wife Della and their boys outside their house in Los Angeles, sometime in the mid-1960s. RIGHT: RC performing at Carnegie Hall in New York City, 1966.

1980s

Sinatra, and Bing Crosby before him, had been a master of words. Ray Charles is a master of sounds. His records disclose

an extraordinary assortment of slurs, glides, turns, shrieks, wails, breaks, shouts, screams, and hollers, all wonderfully

controlled, disciplined by inspired musicianship, and harnessed to ingenious subtleties of harmony, dynamics, and

rhythm. . . It is either the singing of a man whose vocabulary is inadequate to express what is in his heart and mind

or of one whose feelings are too intense for satisfactory verbal or conventionally melodic articulation. He can't tell

it to you. He can't even sing it to you. He has to cry out to you, or shout to you, in tones eloquent of despair—

or exaltation. The voice alone, with little assistance from the text or the notated music, conveys the message.

—Henry Pleasants, *The Great American Popular Singers*, 1985

ABOVE: RC and his longtime friend, Willie Nelson, perform in concert sometime in the 1980s. RIGHT: Among many, many honors, Ray Charles was awarded a star on Hollywood's Walk of Fame in 1981.

Ray Charles stands beside Louis Armstrong, Duke Ellington, and a handful of others among the presiding geniuses of twentieth-century popular music. Five decades of Ray's music pulse in the electric airwaves, music touching millions, soul to soul, every day.

Ray Charles' greatness as a musician began with the abundant musical gifts RC Robinson was given at birth, yet those gifts grew only because, boy and man, Ray labored to perfect them. Endless practice made him a jazz pianist of major importance, a superb arranger, and a songwriter who wrote his own breakthrough songs. Unusual intelligence helped him master the many crafts of music making and run a successful business in a competitive marketplace. Dogged determination made him board and de-board countless trains, cars, buses and airplanes, and walk in and out of countless halls and hotels—all to bring his music to the people.

Ray's greatness springs, on the grandest scale, from his total immersion in the musical currents of his time. Listening in the dark, he soaked up sounds and styles from every idiom, and from them wrought a personal idiom more vital than many of its sources. His more intimate greatness lies in his singing voice. Critics have found much to fault Ray for, yet few complain about his singing. What a voice! No other singer in pop comes close to his breath of vocal shadings—falsetto, scream, talk, whisper, croon, laugh, howl, giggle, sob—or his freedom in changing and blending those colors to convey every flicker of evanescent emotion. . . .

"I am with you, and I know how it is," wrote Walt Whitman to future generations from *Brooklyn Bridge*. "Me, too," sang Ray to future generations on *Volcanic Action of My Soul*. Many have felt, and many will always feel, the presence of the man in the music of Ray Charles. Who is this Ray who comes so close to our ears, who enters so swiftly, so pleasingly, so lastingly into our hearts? Someone different to each of us, but someone surely with us—not as substantially, perhaps, as in the flesh, yet by art's magic, vibrantly focused in spirit.

Like many practitioners of this magic, Ray never professed to understand its furthest mysteries. All he could do was to pour himself into making music to the fullest extent of his powers, and that he did day after day all his life. The rest was up to his listeners.

—Michael Lydon, *Ray Charles,* 1998

Long before I knew we had so much in common, I knew him as a man and a voice that touched my heart. His voice made me feel like I wanted to love deeper, to care more and reach out and touch the world.

—Stevie Wonder, *The New York Times,* June 19, 2004

LEFT: Stevie Wonder and Ray Charles during the taping of a benefit at the Pasadena Civic Auditorium on September 20, 1991 in Pasadena, California. ABOVE RIGHT: President and Mrs. Clinton present a National Medal of Arts to RC on October 7, 1993, in Washington, D.C.

2000s

Ray Charles had a refinement of spirit that prevented him from ever singing or playing a false note. He was always, always right. And he was an incredible influence on all the rock and roll artists: on the Beatles, the Rolling Stones, the Who, Van Morrison, Joe Cocker, Eric Clapton, Jeff Beck. They were all Ray Charles fans.

—Ahmet Ertegun, *Rolling Stone,* July 8-22, 2004

Ray Charles breathes life into every note he writes. Also he is an excellent technician. It was Ray who first showed me how to voice sections in writing. He has an uncanny ability to hear things.

—Quincy Jones, *Downbeat,* July 7, 1960

ABOVE: RC performing at the 11th Annual Santa Cruz Blues Festival at Aptos Village Park in California, May 24, 2003. RIGHT: Quincy Jones presents an award to RC at the 35th Annual NAACP Image Awards, March 7, 2004. FAR RIGHT: RC performing at the Mohegan Sun Hotel Grand Opening in June of 2002.

It may be "Crying Time," but clap your hands,
stamp your feet, stand and give God praise!
Thank God for giving us Ray Charles.

—The Rev. Robert Robinson, Sr., son of Ray Charles,
speaking at his father's funeral in Los Angeles,
Friday, June 18, 2004

Ray Charles' annotated sheet music was placed on a piano beside his casket. His funeral was held in Los Angeles on June 18th, 2004.

UNIVERSAL PICTURES
and
BRISTOL BAY PRODUCTIONS
Present
An ANVIL FILMS Production

In Association with
BALDWIN ENTERTAINMENT

A TAYLOR HACKFORD Film

JAMIE FOXX

KERRY WASHINGTON
CLIFTON POWELL
AUNJANUE ELLIS
HARRY LENNIX
TERRENCE DASHON HOWARD
LARENZ TATE

BOKEEM WOODBINE   SHARON WARREN
CURTIS ARMSTRONG   RICHARD SCHIFF
WENDELL PIERCE   CHRIS THOMAS KING
DAVID KRUMHOLTZ   KURT FULLER
WARWICK DAVIS   PATRICK BAUCHAU
ROBERT WISDOM   DENISE DOWSE
And
REGINA KING

Casting by
NANCY KLOPPER, CSA

Costume Designer
SHAREN DAVIS

Music Supervisor
CURT SOBEL

Score Composed by
CRAIG ARMSTRONG

Original and New Recordings by
RAY CHARLES

Edited by
PAUL HIRSCH

Production Designer
STEPHEN ALTMAN

Director of Photography
PAWEL EDELMAN

Line Producer
BARBARA A. HALL

Co-Producers
RAY CHARLES ROBINSON, JR.
ALISE BENJAMIN
NICK MORTON

Executive Producers
WILLIAM J. IMMERMAN   JAIME RUCKER KING

Producers
TAYLOR HACKFORD   STUART BENJAMIN

Producers
HOWARD BALDWIN   KAREN BALDWIN

Story by
TAYLOR HACKFORD and JAMES L. WHITE

Screenplay by
JAMES L. WHITE

Directed by
TAYLOR HACKFORD

THE VISUALIZATION OF *RAY*

by Taylor Hackford

Ray Charles' story was epic in scope. His journey began in the abject poverty of the segregated South where rural blacks still plowed share-cropper plots with mules and very few owned automobiles. By the time Ray's journey ended, he owned his own jet, ran a multimillion-dollar business, was welcomed by heads of state in every corner of the world, and performed in palaces for kings and queens.

After trying to secure financing for nearly thirteen years, my producing partner Stuart Benjamin finally sold *Ray* to Crusader Entertainment (now Bristol Bay Productions), run at that time by Howard Baldwin and financed by Phil Anschutz, and they made it immediately clear that this film would only be made on a modest budget. My problem was that Ray Charles' life needed a big budget "look" because once the teenage Ray left northern Florida, he never stopped moving, literally traveling millions of miles. For the audience to appreciate the enormity of Ray's accomplishment, I knew we'd have to create the illusion that we were traveling those miles with him.

My first creative collaborator was screenwriter Jimmy White, who shared Ray's rural, southern, African-American roots. Jimmy had served in the U.S. Navy so he also had a worldview. Together we framed out the story we wanted to tell, which basically covered thirty-four years of Ray's life from ages five to forty-nine; as I said, an epic story. There was no way that I could afford to shoot the hundreds of cities around the world where Ray had lived and performed. In fact, our budget dictated that we shoot in only one city, which turned out to be New Orleans, Louisiana. (Although I was subsequently able to negotiate a few extra shoot days in Los Angeles at the end of the schedule.)

Enter my next creative collaborator, production designer Stephen Altman. Steve had designed many of Robert Altman's films, and therefore, he was very skilled at putting a high level of production value on the screen

for a limited budget. Steve and I devised a plan to use historical stock footage throughout the film to establish "master shots" of historical scope and detail that we would never be able to shoot on our limited budget. For instance, we used stock shots of cities like Seattle, New York, L.A., Chicago, Paris, and Rome, which contained incredible production values: hundreds of historic buildings, thousands of period cars, and product billboards. Our strategy was to establish each major location with stock shots and then cut into smaller, more contained sets/locations in New Orleans, which Steve had designed to integrate with the original footage. We did major research in advance in order to find the right historical footage that Steve could match to. Some of this stock footage was of extremely poor quality, but advances in digital processing have made it possible to clean up damaged or faded film and transform it into acceptable quality. We "stepped on" (photographically degraded) some of our own footage so that the transitions in and out of these stock shots would be less noticeable.

Steve built several sets for the film: the famously funky Atlantic office/recording studios and Ray's myriad hotel rooms. He and our set decorator, Maria Nay, also adapted many actual New Orleans and Los Angeles locations into terrifically evocative period sets. One of my favorites was Jellyroll, the tiny African-American enclave on the Georgia/Florida border where Ray grew up. We transformed an old plantation on the outskirts of Thibodeaux, Louisiana, hauling in tons of red Georgia dirt to re-create the look of Ray's childhood. Steve and Maria created another bit of magic when they transformed the long-closed Louisiana Scottish Rite Masonic Temple into Sam Clark's ABC-Paramount Records office. They also redesigned many New Orleans bars and clubs into locations that beautifully evoked the Chitlin' Circuit of the late forties and early fifties.

Another invaluable collaborator on the team was cinematographer Pavel Edelman who was making his first film in the U.S. I'd seen Pavel's work in Poland where he collaborated with one of my favorite directors, Andrej Wajda. Like most of us, Pavel had been a huge Ray Charles fan growing up, but unlike the rest of us, he'd had to scrounge for "underground" copies of Ray's records in Poland. I spent many hours with Pavel discussing the "photographic looks" of *Ray*. I use the plural "looks," because I wanted different visualizations for each of the three separate levels of reality in the film:

1. The Linear Story that follows Ray's evolution as an artist;
2. Ray's Flashbacks that show actual events in his childhood; and
3. Ray's Visions of Aretha, which are psychological dream/nightmares of his mother speaking to him at crucial moments in his life.

Usually, filmmakers will photograph their linear, "real time" sequences in natural colors and then de-saturate or mute their flashbacks. We reversed that equation, deciding to use a de-saturated bleach bypass for the linear story and a natural color look for the flashbacks. Actually, even our "natural colors" were ultra-saturated, almost hyper-real. Because Ray was born sighted, I wanted to communicate how vibrant the colors must have seemed to him on his first spring day. Pavel photographed the entire film without special processing, because we decided to create these "separate looks" in post-production using the Digital Intermediate process. (The "Aretha Visions" became almost monochromatic "solarizations.") However, this deferral of the colorization presented problems for Stephen Altman, Maria Nay, and our costume designer, Sharen Davis. They had to "turn-up" the color quotient on their sets and costumes so that our de-saturating didn't destroy their designs. Although we did several tests so that all the department heads could experiment in advance with their color palettes, there were times when we'd arrive at a set and discover that the paint on the walls was extremely vibrant. At those moments I could hear Pavel mumble: "Altman has gone mad," but ultimately Steve knew that Pavel would have control of the final color in the Digital Intermediate process, and obviously he did.

Pavel and I also worked out a strategy for camera movement. In the flashbacks the only world little Ray knew was Jellyroll, so his life is totally stable. Thus, there is very little camera movement in the flashbacks; it's almost as if the camera is rooted in the red earth of Georgia. However, when Ray gets on that Greyhound bus and travels across America, the camera starts moving and never stops, just like Ray's life. In the early scenes we used dollies and cranes, which provided smooth, steady movement. Then, when Ray meets and marries Della the camera temporarily slows down, because she provided stability for him. As Ray's ambition/ego heats up, and his use of heroin accelerates, we switched to hand-held cameras to show that his life was becoming more and more unstable. At the end of the film when Ray kicks heroin and resolves his relationship with his mother and brother, the camera finally slows down and stops. Normally, neither Pavel nor I like to call attention to our camera technique, but in this instance, I think it helped illustrate Ray's emotional journey.

I already mentioned Sharen Davis, our costume designer, but she deserves special recognition for her contributions. In a period film, the costumes and hairstyles are among the most important elements in defining the look of the film. Ray Charles was always a classy dresser, and Sharen designed many original outfits for Jamie that I believe did justice to RC's sartorial splendor. She also had great fun redesigning and turning up the color for the Raelettes' costumes. However, making costumes for the principal cast was not Sharen's biggest problem. The culture depicted in our film was almost entirely African-American. Blacks may not have had much money when Ray Charles first started performing, but they were never wanting for style. When people went out on a weekend to a club on the Chitlin' Circuit, they dressed up and looked terrific. It was important to both Sharen and me that our extras had that same high level of style. Her problem was that she had to dress hundreds and hundreds of extras. Certainly, Barbara Hall, our line producer, was sympathetic, but although she may have wanted to extend Sharen's budget, there wasn't much money to give. How Sharen and her staff managed to find those wonderful costumes and fit all those extras on her meager budget is a miracle.

Normally, the editor is not considered to be a part of the visual design team, but in this instance, Paul Hirsch contributed mightily to the "look" of *Ray*.

Paul came on board our project nearly two months late and immediately went to work in Los Angeles cutting the film that I'd shot in New Orleans. I didn't see any of his work until after the film was completed so when I walked into his editing room, my shoulders were tense with dread, but after viewing only two minutes of his cut, I immediately relaxed. It was terrific. I had always planned to lace Ray's music throughout the narrative, using his songs to propel the story forward, and Paul had understood exactly what I'd intended. He'd cut several incredible montages that are both beautiful to view and, more importantly, economical revelations of both narrative and character. His use of soft-edged wipes for both montages and transitions added a stylish fluidity to the "look" of *Ray*. Working with him daily in the editing room was an incredibly stimulating and productive experience.

On this film I desperately needed a 2nd unit director who could pick up elements I'd designed but didn't have time to shoot with the 1st unit. I asked my long-time storyboard artist Raymond Prado to join us in this capacity and he dove in with alacrity. Not only was Raymond already in my head (we'd designed many sequences together including the title treatment), but he also suggested many other wonderful shots that ended up in the film. Since we didn't have the money to hire thousands of extras to fill the larger auditoriums and theaters that RC grew into as he became more famous, Raymond filmed only two hundred extras, moving them from one section to another, changing their clothing and hairstyles, and getting them to demonstrate that fantastic energy that Ray engendered in his audiences. We then combined these individual sections digitally in postproduction. This technique is called Digital Tiling, and it's very precise. Ray's work was impeccable. He was given his own photographic team, and they were constantly shooting montage material (neon signs, buses on country roads, etc.) that ended up in Paul Hirsh's fantastic montages. It was wonderful to watch my long-time protégé step so effectively into a new creative category.

I had many other collaborators who contributed mightily to the "look" of *Ray*: Stacye Branch, head of the make-up department; LaLette Littlejohn, who spent long hours applying Jamie's prosthetic eyes; Joanne Stafford-Chaney and Paul Anthony-Morris, our key hair stylists; property master Tony Maccario who researched and found all the terrific period instruments used in the film; and Welch Lambeth, our transportation coordinator, whose staff scrounged all over Louisiana for our fabulous period cars and buses.

THE NON-VISUALIZATION

Finally, I must mention two other collaborators whose work was vital to this film: line producer Barbara Hall and casting director Nancy Klopper.

Nancy has worked with me since *An Officer and a Gentleman* and is like a member of my family. She has incredible instincts, and I trust her taste implicitly. We often argue intensely about casting choices, and occasionally she's right (my attempt at humor). Nancy did a masterful job on this film with assistance from location casting director Mark Fincannon and extras casting manager (New Orleans) Shirley Fulton Crumley.

Collaborating with Barbara Hall was a new experience for me. (Actually, except for Curt Sobel, Raymond Prado, and Nancy Klopper, all of my collaborators on this film were new colleagues for me.) Both Stuart and I worked intensely with Barbara to fit the budget into Crusader Entertainment's stringent requirements. (Make no mistake, both Phil and Howard were incredibly brave and generous, but they were also astute businessmen and knew that this film had to be made at the right price to stand a chance in today's marketplace.) Luckily, they were also passionate fans of Ray Charles, and with Barbara's tireless work we were finally able to get them to give us a green light. (By the way it also helped that we made the film in Louisiana where a piece of recently passed tax incentive legislation allowed us to save several million dollars. There had been initial talk of taking this project to Canada, but we strongly resisted that possibility, and happily, the entire production was made in the U.S.)

These people and so many more contributed their talents to making this an unforgettable filmmaking experience for me, and I am deeply grateful to them all.